Tuttle Public Library
PO Box 383
305 W Main St
Tuttle, OK 73089

MOTE

M·O·T·E

CHAP REAVER

Delacorte Press

Published by
Delacorte Press
Bantam Doubleday Dell Publishing Group, Inc.
666 Fifth Avenue
New York, New York 10103

Library of Congress Cataloging in Publication Data

Reaver, Herbert R.
    Mote / by Herbert R. Reaver.
        p.   cm.
    Summary: When their friend Mote is accused of murdering a
schoolteacher, two teenage boys decide to do everything they can to
clear his name.
    ISBN 0-385-30163-4
    [1. Mystery and detective stories.   2. Friendship—Fiction.]
I. Title.
PZ7.R23767Mo   1990
[Fic]—dc20   90-2817
                                                      CIP
                                                       AC

Manufactured in the United States of America

October 1990

10 9 8 7 6 5 4 3 2 1

BVG

FOR DIXIE

▲ *1* ▲

I WAS EARLY for my eight-o'clock appointment with the principal, Mr. Reeves. I knew I would have to wait but got there early anyway. You always had to wait for these kinds of appointments. It was part of the routine to let you know how much more important the principal was than you were. I sat in the hard oak chair and watched Miss Cavendish type. She could really type fast and had no breasts at all.

The minute hand clicked to eight o'clock. I looked at the door to Mr. Reeves's office. It didn't open and I decided not to look at it anymore. I knew that when it did open I would get that feeling in my chest, like my heart had bumped up against something, the same feeling I had the night before when the detectives came to my front door.

There were two of them. They had brought my best friend Billy over to my house to question us about Mote. The white detective was big and heavy, with an unfortunate hairpiece that was a shade lighter than his natural hair. Maybe he was supposed to gray into it. The black detective was about six feet four with a slender, athletic build that made me think basketball. Billy and I were glad to tell them everything we knew. We figured the more they knew about Mote, the more they would realize that he couldn't have done such a thing. We had heard about the murder at school. Everybody was talking about it.

We sat around our kitchen table, answering the detectives'

questions. The white detective said, "And you got no idea where this Mote guy come from?"

He pronounced *idea* like it was *idear*. I said, "No, sir."

The detective kept looking at me. He had a way of doing that. After you answered his questions he would just keep looking at you.

"I mean, he never said where he was from. He talked about a lot of places he's been, but he never said he was from someplace."

He stared at me some more and when I didn't say anything he looked at Billy. Billy said, "That's right. He never said to me where he was from either. Just places he'd been." The detective kept looking at Billy and it must have bothered him too.

"Florida," Billy said. "He went to Florida a lot."

The detective looked at me and stared for a minute. He kept a scowl on his face. "How old are you?"

"Seventeen," I said. He gave me some more look. "I mean, I'll be seventeen next month." What he probably did was work on his look, practice it in the mirror while he was alone at home.

The big detective nodded to the black detective. He opened a bag and dumped some pieces of wood onto our kitchen table. Then the big detective said, "Do you recognize any of this wood?"

"Yes, sir." I pointed to a piece of walnut with some pencil marks on it. "That one there. Mote was going to carve a porpoise out of it."

"A purpose?"

"A porpoise. You know, a dolphin. Mote read books about dolphins."

Some more look. I imagined him working on it, practicing tough looks in his bathroom mirror, and it didn't bother me as much. I didn't have a mean look of my own to give back to him, so I gave him my innocent, sincere one. It didn't faze him.

"And you don't know his last name?"

"No, sir. We just call him Mote."

We went over the description and the black detective wrote in a small notepad. Mote was about forty, a little under six feet tall, with a muscular build. His hair was brown with a few scattered gray hairs mixed in. "He has a scar under his left eye," I said, "exactly like mine."

The black detective looked at me. "What you call that, a moon scar?"

"Yeah, more like a crescent moon."

"Me too." He touched under his eye. "When I was a kid they used to call me Moon."

"Maybe we're all some kind of soul brothers," I said.

The black detective grinned.

The fat detective said, "Any other scars, tattoos, or birthmarks?"

"No, sir."

He looked at Billy and Billy shook his head.

The big detective loosened his tie and unbuttoned his collar. "Okay, I want to start at the beginning, when you first met this Mote character." He pointed at Billy. "You start out." He looked at me. "If he forgets something, you break in. Don't leave out nothin'."

"Anything," I said. "You mean don't leave out *anything*."

The black detective coughed into his hand and looked away. The big detective gave me some more of his mean look. "You know what I mean."

Billy started off by telling about the scaffolding. His uncle was a painter and had just finished a job on a big three-story house. They had all this scaffolding left over and Billy asked if we could have it. We wanted to build a clubhouse.

That was four years ago, in May. Billy's uncle had dumped the scaffolding up by the railroad tracks, about two blocks from where we lived. Billy and I borrowed hammers and went up to the tracks one Saturday to start pulling nails and sorting the lumber.

Mote had come walking up from the creek, drying his hair with a towel. He stood a few yards away, watching us work.

He had on jeans, running shoes without socks, and was bare-chested. I said, "Good morning."

Mote smiled. "Morning," he said, and walked up to us, combing his fingers through his hair.

"So we just stood around and talked," Billy said. "He asked us what we were going to build and said we had some real good wood there. After a while he asked us if we would like some coffee and we went down to his camp and sat around a while. He had a neat little camp set up by the creek."

The big detective looked at me. "You got any coffee?"

"I can make some," I said. "Instant."

"Instant's okay."

I got up and found a pot, filled it with water, and put it on a burner, on High. I set four cups and spoons on the table, along with a sugar bowl and a jar of Folgers. The cups didn't match and the big detective took the largest one. I poured some milk into a pitcher.

We spooned coffee crystals into our cups. Mote had taught me to drink coffee black, the grounds boiled in a blue enamel pot. The big detective put in three spoons of sugar and it made the back of my throat feel gummy. I figured he was going to get even dumber when the sugar hit his bloodstream.

He said, "So how long did this Mote guy stick around?"

I said, "About three weeks. I don't think he planned to be here that long but he stayed anyway, until we got the clubhouse finished."

Mote knew a lot about building. He knew a lot about everything. Billy and I did all the actual work, but Mote told us what to do next and how to do it. We worked on it every day after school until dark. Mote explained everything as we went along and talked to us like we were grown men.

Billy's uncle had given us some cans of leftover paint. There was a half gallon of Colonial White and other cans with small amounts of blue, yellow, green, pink, and gray. We stirred it all together and gave the clubhouse two coats. It was kind of an ugly green. The paint didn't mix very well and there were some flecks of pink and white in it. We called it Colonial Puke and thought it was a pretty clever name. Billy and I repeated it a lot, "Colonial Puke," back and forth to each other.

On the day we put on the final coat, Mote cooked a dinner for us. We had fresh-caught fish cooked over hickory wood, with corn roasted in the coals, with the shucks on. Mote had pulled some cattails from the creek and steamed the roots like asparagus. There was a dandelion salad and wild mushrooms to go with the fish. Mote could always put together great-tasting meals from wild foods he'd gathered, even weeds. He showed us how to find and cook the stuff and taught us the names. Things like lamb's-quarter, hickory jacks, field cress, and dock. He called it hobo food.

After we ate, Mote made coffee. We climbed the bank with our cups and sat in our clubhouse. Billy and I were proud of it and happy that it was finished. It was ten feet by fifteen feet, built like a regular house, except smaller. Mote didn't like to be in the clubhouse with the door closed. It made him nervous or something. He sat in the doorway and Billy and I sat on the floor, admiring our shack in silence until Mote said, "I guess I'll be taking off tomorrow." I had been afraid he was going to say that and it took all the happiness out of the clubhouse being finished.

Billy asked, "Where you heading, Mote?"

"Up north. Maine, Vermont. I'll probably work my way up to Canada around August and come back through Michigan. The Upper Peninsula."

"Fishing?" I asked.

"Yeah. Fishing, selling my flies, my knives, swapping stories, hanging around." When he sipped his coffee there were laugh wrinkles at the corner of his eyes. "Not a very responsible life for a grown man."

"Sounds pretty good to me," I said.

Billy said, "There's good fishing around here."

Mote said, "I know, Billy. But I have to keep moving."

A whippoorwill tuned up across the creek. I said, "Will you come back to see us, Mote?"

"Sure. I'll swing back through in the fall. What you guys can be doing, you can be on the lookout for a used oil drum. I'll come back and show you how to rig up a wood stove. Not the big fifty-five-gallon drum." He held his hands up, about two feet apart. "The smaller size."

The big detective asked if he could have some more coffee and I poured him some more. I thought about handing him a scoop for the sugar bowl, but he managed with his spoon. Four spoonfuls this time. I glanced at the black detective and caught him watching me watching the fat detective. He rolled his eyes and made a funny face.

"Did Mote come back that fall?"

Billy said, "Yes, sir. He came back and helped us make a wood stove, just like he said he would. It worked real well. Still does. Even when it gets below freezing we can light a fire and be warm in about ten minutes. Twenty minutes and you have to take off your jacket. Mote set up all his fly-tying stuff on an old table we found."

Mote stayed about a week. We tried to get him to stay inside the shack, but he said he couldn't get to sleep inside four walls. He taught Billy and me how to tie flies. Mote was really good, and fast. He could tie about fifty flies an hour after he got everything set up. I could do about three and they came out looking like little feather dusters. Mote was patient with us. He encouraged us to keep trying and before long we started to get the hang of it. We took a few flies down to the creek and caught some bluegills, using Mote's fly rod. I had always used worms before and this was more fun. Mote said he had never seen anyone catch on to fly casting as quickly as Billy and I had. Mote did that kind of thing a lot, acting like he was amazed at how smart and clever Billy and I were. Sometimes I knew he was exaggerating, but I liked it anyway. After he left I missed him a lot.

Mote came back the next May, then again in September. He came in May and September each year after that. He just hung out with us for a few days each time and we tied flies, went fishing, and talked. We talked about everything.

The big detective said, "When did you start having trouble with the victim?"

"Mr. Holder?"

"Yeah."

I groaned and palmed my face, a gesture I had picked up from Mote. "Mr. Holder and I, we never got along very well. When I was a little kid, about ten or so, he taught our Sunday school class and, well, he would say things I didn't understand and when I asked him about it, it would make him mad. He'd say, 'Maybe you should teach the class, Miller. You're so smart.' Stuff like that."

I sipped my coffee. "Well, after that he didn't like me much and picked on me all the time. At least I thought he did and I would ask questions just to bug him. Then one Sunday he was talking about going to heaven, about how *only* Christians who believed in the Bible could go there, and I got to thinking again. I should have known better."

The black detective said, "What happened?"

"It was something I used to wonder about anyway, so I raised my hand. When he called on me I asked, 'What about people who never hear about Jesus or ever see a Bible? Like some guy who lives in a jungle. What happens to him when he dies?'

"Well, Mr. Holder walked over to me, put his face real close, and said, 'He goes straight to hell.' He had his teeth clenched and his mouth all puckered up, and I laughed at him. I laughed at him because I was scared, but some of the other kids laughed too and you could tell he didn't like it. He told me I better get all those Communist ideas out of my head, or I'd be going to hell too, along with the jungle bunny."

The black detective looked up. *"Jungle bunny?"*

"Yeah, that's what he said."

The black detective smiled, a big one. "He ever say *nigger?*"

"Yes, sir."

"*Coon?* He ever say that?"

"Uh-huh."

"*Spook?*"

"No, sir. I don't think so."

The big detective said, "Quit clowning around, Ed." He turned to me. "Did this Mote guy know about the church-school business?"

I said, "*Jigaboo.* He said *jigaboo* sometimes. 'Too many jigaboos in professional basketball,' he used to say."

The black detective laughed.

The white detective said, "How about it, did Mote know about all that?"

"Yeah. Yes, sir. We got to talking about religion and I told Mote about it. Told him that's why I didn't go to church anymore, 'cause I had decided that I was going to have to figure religion out for myself. I couldn't depend on anyone else to do my thinking for me, especially guys like Mr. Holder."

The big detective nodded his head, with his lips pushed out. "And that's when Mote started to get it in for Holder, huh?"

"No, sir. Mote thought it was funny. He got a kick out of it."

"Why's that?"

"I'm not real sure. Mote just said that Holder had done me a real favor. I think he meant something about not being afraid to do your own thinking."

The black detective walked over and laid his empty cup in the sink and turned the burner up to High under the water. The big detective said, "What was the trouble about in school?"

I took a sip of coffee, groaned, and rubbed my face. "That happened two days ago," I said. "But it really goes back to the church stuff.

"Mr. Holder works for my dad—he used to work for my dad—he's a draftsman and Dad says he's pretty good. Well, I wanted to take mechanical drawing in high school this year. I knew Mr. Holder would be the teacher, but I figured we could get along all right. It's just one day a week. Mr. Holder isn't a . . . he wasn't a regular teacher—he just had that one class a week."

The big detective twisted around to take a gray handkerchief out of his hip pocket. He looked inside several folds before he found an empty slot. After he blew his nose he took a quick peek to see what it looked like.

I said, "Mr. Holder had this trick of digging his thumb into your elbow joint and finding your funny bone. It really hurt. He would have something set up at the front of the class, a block of wood or some machine part that we were supposed to draw, and he would walk around and look at our work. If you had something wrong, Mr. Holder would walk you up to the front of the room, digging into your funny bone, and make you look at the model real close. He did it to everybody a time or two, but he got to doing me every time, sometimes twice, even when I didn't have anything wrong with my drawing. We had tennis practice after his class and my arm would be sore and numb.

"So Wednesday I had a match after school. The city tournament, and I wanted to play. I won the tournament last year." I glanced up at the detectives. They weren't impressed. "So I went up to Mr. Holder before class and asked him to please lay off my arm that day. I explained it to him as nice as I could. I even asked him just to do my left arm if he felt that it was something he just had to do.

"Mr. Holder said. 'Can't take it, huh? Little sissy tennis player.'

"I said, 'Yeah, I am a sissy. Just please leave me alone for one day,' but he didn't. A few minutes after class started he came around and tried to grab my arm. I backed away from him, and I swear, he went kind of crazy and chased me around the room until he got me cornered. His eyes were all bugged out and everything. He grabbed my arm really hard, and I jerked free and just hit him."

The big detective said, "Where did you hit him?"

"In the face," I said. "Made his nose bleed."

The black detective said, "Holder a pretty big dude."

"Yeah," I said. "It was just a lucky punch and I was scared, adrenaline or something." I took another sip of coffee and noticed that my hand was shaking. The black detective poured some boiling water in my cup and I stirred in some coffee crystals. I didn't want any more coffee, but it was something to do.

The big detective said, "So that's why Mr. Holder wanted to have you expelled, huh?"

"Yeah."

"And you told Mote about it?"

"Yes, sir. I'm supposed to see the principal about it tomorrow. Eight o'clock in the morning."

The white detective said, "Show 'em the knife. Ed."

The black detective took a plastic bag out of his coat pocket and laid it on the table. There was a knife inside the bag, the kind that Mote made out of old saw blades. "That Mote's knife?"

Billy groaned and rubbed his face. "Looks like it."

The white detective said, "That's the murder weapon. It looks like Mote went over to Mr. Holder's house and killed him for you."

▲ 2 ▲

THE BIG detective pulled some papers out of his inside coat pocket. "We got a make on your friend, the guy you call Mote. Got his fingerprints from your shack."

The black detective handed Billy the combination lock from our shack. "Had to break it," he said. "Sorry."

The big detective unfolded the papers. "His name's Matthew Oliver Thomas."

I said, "Mote!"

Billy said, "Yeah."

The big detective said, "Huh?"

"His initials," I said. "Mote."

The big detective looked at me with his mouth open. The sugar must have just hit his brain.

The black detective said, "His initials, Lieutenant. M.O.T. You could pronounce that *Mote*."

He still didn't get it. "Well, anyway, you got most of the description right, except for his hair and the scar." He turned a page. "Born in '45, in Hartford, Connecticut. Five eleven. Two years at Brown University, drafted in '65. Wounded in Vietnam. Spent three months in a 'Nam prison camp and got tortured some before he escaped." He turned another page. "Must've come out a little psycho. Three months in a mental hospital. Got a Purple Heart." He looked up. "I thought you guys said he didn't have no scars."

Billy said, "*Any* scars."

I said, "Where was he wounded?"

"Vietnam."

"I mean where on his body?"

The big detective read from the papers. "Three-inch well-healed scar, lateral aspect of right buttock."

I thought a moment. "I don't think I ever saw Mote naked."

Billy said, "Me neither."

"Yeah, maybe. How about his hair though? Says here his hair is white."

I looked at Billy. He said, "You know, Mote's hair was . . . he had more gray in it when we first met him. It seemed to get darker every year. Remember, Chris? We used to tease him about it, accuse him of putting color on it."

The detective leafed through the papers until he found the page he wanted. "His induction physical says his hair is brown." He found another page and read it. "Discharge papers say his hair is white." He looked up from the papers and frowned. "Don't make sense."

I was trying to figure it out. Billy said, "What would make someone's hair turn white like that?"

The black detective made a grunting sound.

It made my head hurt, a dull pain over my eyes.

The white detective shrugged. "Well, anyway, he knows how to kill. Special Forces in 'Nam, a couple decorations. Honorable discharge, no arrests. Sort of dropped out of sight. No record on him after '69." He put the papers back in his pocket.

I took a pack of chewing gum out of my pocket. The big detective said, "Can I have some of that?" and I handed him a stick.

He unwrapped the stick of gum and put it in his mouth. I offered the pack to the black detective and he shook his head. "No, thanks." He watched me closely for a moment. "You didn't know about Vietnam, did you?"

I said, "No."

The big detective said, "I gotta use the toilet."

I walked into the hall with the big detective and pointed to the bathroom. He handed me a business card that said Lt. Frank Baker, and headed for the bathroom while he worked with his belt.

Billy was talking with the black detective in the kitchen. The black detective looked good in his suit, quick and agile even standing still. I figured him for a point guard at a small college. I put the cups and spoons in the sink. The detective held out a card. It said Edward Stienert, Detective.

I said, "Are you guys doing the good cop, bad cop routine?"

Stienert smiled. "No, I really am the good cop."

I said, "Where did you play basketball?"

"Eastern Kentucky."

"Guard?"

"Small forward," he said. "Should have played guard."

I nodded. I loved it when I got that kind of thing right.

The big detective walked in, zipping his fly. "Boy," he said. "I drank all that coffee and he gave me a piece of chewing gum. That hit me, that juice on that sweet . . ." He snapped his fingers. "That triggered me, just like that. Had a terrific BM in there."

After Baker and Stienert left, Billy helped me clean up. We worked quietly, busy with our own thoughts. Billy put away the cups. He knew where everything went in my house, just like I did in his house next door.

Billy said, "Mote ever say anything to you about Vietnam?"

"No, not a word." I pulled the strainer and watched the soapsuds whirlpool down the drain. Billy followed me into the bathroom. "Who do you think could have killed Holder?"

"I don't know." I took off my shirt and threw it in the laundry hamper. "Why don't you spend the night? We'll talk."

I left the shower running for Billy and toweled off in my bedroom. The ten-o'clock news featured Holder's murder. "Today's brutal slaying . . ." I tried the FM station. The announcer was talking about the new Madonna record he was about to play. I turned him off and put on a Ray Charles tape. I love Ray Charles.

Billy came in, drying his back. I said, "You remember what Mote said about the two ways people think?"

Billy said, "Yeah . . . Something about inductive and subjective."

"Inductive and *deductive*," I said. "I don't remember which is which though." I hung my head over the edge of the bunk to look at Billy. We had held lots of conversations in this position over the years. "Mote said most people decide how things are and then spend the rest of their lives looking for proof that they're right. Other people try to examine the evidence and then figure it out."

Mote did that a lot—talked about the way people think. I asked him which way is better and he said neither one was better. They were just different.

"Baker's made up his mind," I said. "He's decided that Mote is guilty and he's not going to look for anything else. He's just going to build up his case against Mote."

Billy said, "He's already got a good case, the knife and and all. Mote running away."

I said, "It must be somebody who knew about Mote. Knew about our clubhouse and Mote's knives."

"Yeah, it could be."

I heard Billy rustle the covers and stand up. He leaned his elbows on my bunk. "Hey, Chris?"

"What?" I could see his eyes in the dark.

"The killer might be somebody we know."

I rolled over on my back and stared at the ceiling. "Sometimes you know what I feel like?"

"What's that?"

"I never told anybody this before, but sometimes I feel like a disc. A big round disc, like a checker—only bigger, about four inches across and smooth, without those little ridges that hold the kinged men together."

Billy said, "What are you talking about?"

"And there's some big guy somewhere. I mean *big*, not like six feet but big like the sky or the mountains. He's playing with these little plastic discs and moving them around and playing with them. It's his game."

"You're crazy, Chris."

"No, listen." I rolled onto my stomach and hung my head over the side so I could look at Billy. "You're a disc too, just like me. Our pictures are inside the discs, like laminated or something. And this big guy, he rolls the dice or spins a pointer and it says Chris Gets Kicked Out of School or Billy Gets Married or Holder Gets Murdered. And, the thing is, the discs like you and me, we think we're real. We think we are deciding what to do and we worry about things and try to make things happen a certain way and it really doesn't matter."

"Like some big Monopoly board, huh?"

"Uh-huh, and we're all the tokens that the Big Guy's moving around."

Billy was quiet for a moment. "I don't believe that," he said. "But there is something crazy that I think sometimes."

"What's that?"

"Sometimes I wonder if I'm the only one who's real, you know, the only one who feels all this stuff, is aware of all the different feelings and moods. I mean, does everybody feel the way I do?"

I said, "Like what?"

"Well, I guess it's like your Big-Guy-in-the-Sky thing, in a way. But I wonder . . . I imagine that everything is just props. Like, I'm real but everything else is just make-believe stuff."

"I'm real, Billy. Believe me."

"Yeah, I know. I guess everybody is. I mean, to themselves they're more real than anything. Everybody probably feels like they are right at the center of the universe."

We were quiet for several minutes. Billy said, "When I try to think of people and imagine how they feel, what they're thinking and feeling, it makes me like them more."

"What do you mean?"

"Well," Billy said. "Like you. When I think about you and what you must be feeling and wondering about. When I think that you must want certain things and worry about some things, it makes me think that you are just like me—on the inside you're just like me and it makes me like you more. It makes me feel closer to you and I want everything to go right for you."

I thought about Mote and wondered where he was and what he was thinking. Mote used to talk about how most people were self-centered and cared little for anything or anyone except themselves.

I leaned over the top bunk. Billy turned his head to look at me. I said, "Is your mind going all the time?"

Billy said, "Uh-huh. You mean like a conversation?"

"Yeah, this dialogue that's always running."

"And pictures," Billy said. "Sometimes I think in pictures and words together. I can hear the words and see the pictures. You think everyone does that?"

"I don't know."

There was a whippoorwill singing out the back window. He must have been real young or something and didn't have the song down right. *"Weahwheel, weahwheel,"* he said.

Billy said, "What could have happened to Mote that made his hair turn white?"

"I don't know." I got the pain over my eyes again. "Mote always talked about our problems. You know that? We never talked about his."

"Yeah."

I felt the bunk move as Billy shifted position. "So what are you going to do tomorrow, Chris?"

"I don't know. See what the Big Guy spins, I guess."

▲ *3* ▲

AT EIGHT-FOURTEEN I was staring at the door to the principal's office when it opened. Detective Stienert walked out first, then Mr. Reeves. Stienert winked at me, then turned to shake hands.

Mr. Reeves told me to have a seat in his office. He was a short, stocky man, about five feet six. His hair was mostly white, short like a soldier's. He sat behind his desk and began reading from a file. He had a lot of plaques on his walls.

He cleared his throat. "This is a very unpleasant matter, isn't it, Chris?"

"Yes, sir."

"Ordinarily, striking a teacher results in automatic expulsion. You understand that?"

"Yes, sir. I do. Sure."

He fooled around with the papers in the folder some more. "But apparently there were some extenuating circumstances. Some provocation." He looked at me over his glasses. "Not that I can ever condone striking a teacher."

"No, sir. Definitely not."

"Nor can I condone the unauthorized use of corporal punishment by our teachers. If you had brought Mr. Holder's actions to my attention, I would have put a stop to it."

"Yes, sir. I should have."

"Didn't want to be a tattletale, did you?"

"Uh . . . I guess that's part of it."

17

"Were you afraid I would take the teacher's side?"

"No, sir. Everybody knows that you're real fair. It's just . . . I mean, I really didn't even think of it."

Mr. Reeves took off his glasses and pinched the corners of his eyes. "I wonder why." He smiled at me. "Sometimes I think I'm the last person to learn what's going on in this school."

"It must be a tough job, being a principal."

From the way he looked at me I knew I had just scored a point. "It can be at times," he said.

He put his glasses back on. "Let's do it this way: I'm not going to take any disciplinary action against you. This won't appear on your record."

"Thanks, Mr. Reeves."

"But anything that goes on in this school that I should know about, I want you to come and see me."

"I will, sir."

He got up from his chair. I stood and we shook hands across the desk. He said, "What did you hit him with?"

"A straight left."

There was a low-pitched hum in the hallway instead of the usual shouts and clatter. Little groups of students were clustered together in intense conversations. They became silent and stared at me as I went down the hall. I could feel them watching me as I passed and it was hard to walk normally, like I was wading through warm molasses.

Billy and I had decided that the killer could be anyone in school, another teacher, or even someone from our neighborhood. Anyone who knew about Mote's knives. Billy said even I was a suspect. I reminded him that we had been together in class on Thursday morning, and he looked disappointed.

Billy is smart, but he makes real dumb mistakes like that when he tries to think too fast. He is a slow, steady thinker and ends up knowing more about things than I do. It just takes him longer. We make an interesting pair. I catch on to things fast, learn in a hurry, then get bored and move on to something else. Billy is slow to grasp a new idea and a lot of people think he's stupid. He isn't.

Mote had noticed the difference in our thinking speeds. He told Billy that he would probably go farther in life than I would, because of his determination and the way he kept at something until he got it all figured out. I had told Billy the same thing, but it seemed to mean more to him, coming from Mote. He wasn't afraid to ask questions in class after that, even though he knew that some of the kids would laugh at him.

Mote used to fuss at me in that half-teasing way he had about how I just coasted through school, getting B's when I could have gotten A's by studying once in a while. I don't take criticism very well. When people point out my faults it makes me feel terrible, like nobody likes me and nobody ever will. But Mote could do it without making me feel bad. He always let me know that he liked me the way I was.

Billy was waiting for me in the hall outside our English classroom. He said, "How did you make out with Mr. Reeves?"

"All right," I said. "Stienert had talked to him."

We took our seats. Mr. Douglas came in and called the roll. He paused and looked up when he called my name and again when he called Billy's. Mr. Douglas was a tall red-haired guy with a bad temper who went berserk now and then. Last winter, when the faculty played the varsity basketball team, Mr. Douglas had started a fistfight with the kid who was guarding him. He used to sit with Mr. Holder in the lunchroom too. I opened my notebook and wrote SUSPECTS at the top of a page. Then I wrote: 1. Douglas. Hothead. Knew Holder.

By the end of the day I had twenty-two names on my sheet. It felt strange to think about people I knew and try to imagine them killing Holder. I read the names to Billy as we walked to his house. His mother was in the kitchen. She was almost always in the kitchen.

Billy's mom looks like Karl Malden. She fixed us sand-wiches and asked about my meeting with Mr. Reeves. I told her that everything came out all right and watched her face. The worried frown changed to a smile and her shoulders relaxed.

Billy's father was killed in an auto accident when Billy was twelve and his mother had never remarried, devoting her entire attention to Billy. Mom and I had gone to the funeral and I still remembered how hard Billy had cried. When they lowered the coffin into the grave our eyes met over the top of the coffin. There was so much pain in Billy's face that it made me start crying too. It was the first time that I cried without being ashamed of it. Something happened to us as we watched each other crying across the open grave. Some-thing that joined us in a special friendship. We never talked about it.

I always wondered about the way Mote had showed up shortly after Billy's father was killed and my father moved out after the divorce. The Big Guy in the Sky had given us a great spin.

Billy and his mom had received a lot of money from the insurance settlement, and she didn't have to work. Billy and I had tried to fix her up with dates, but she always said she wasn't very interested. The men weren't all that interested either. A man can look like Karl Malden and get away with it. For a woman it's a tough break.

After we ate, Billy and I got the lawn mower and weed whacker out of his shed. Friday was our grass-cutting day and we did both lawns together. I was putting gas in the mower when Billy said, "Pull the spark-plug wire off."

"Huh?"

"Pull the spark-plug wire off. Leon's coming."

Leon came walking up, grinning like always. He was a big black guy of twenty-two or twenty-three. He had the mind of a ten-year-old and was stuck there. His hands were shoved into the pockets of his baggy pants. He had on orange boots without socks, a sweatshirt with the sleeves cut off, and a cap that said Russia Sucks. His thick glasses were off-center and it made his face look lopsided.

"Hey, Leon," Billy said.

Leon said, "Hey."

"We can't get this lawn mower started," I said. "I think it's ruined. Probably have to throw it away and get a new one."

Leon looked at the lawn mower and frowned. He unscrewed the cap and saw that there was gas in it. Then he pulled the start rope and worked the choke.

Billy said, "It's no use, Leon. We've tried everything."

Leon shook the lawn mower and looked at it some more. He finally saw the loose spark-plug wire and connected it. He stood back and crossed his arms over his chest. "Now try it."

It started right up. Billy worked the throttle, making it roar for a moment before he shut it off. "How did you do that, Leon?"

Leon laughed and clapped his hands. "Land sakes," he said. "Land sakes, you guys are dumb." Leon had a theory about why Billy and I had so little common sense. "You reads too many books," he said.

I straightened Leon's glasses for him.

Billy started mowing while I worked the weed whacker. Leon sat on my porch and studied his driver's-education manual. He had been studying the manual and failing the written driver's test once a month for five years, ever since he bought his car. He had a 1980 Toyota with ten thousand miles on it in his garage. He let me drive it now and then and would wash, wax, and change the oil after my short trips.

We finished Billy's yard and started on mine. Mrs. Crowly, our neighbor on the other side, watched us from her front porch. I waved at her and she waved back. Mrs. Crowly was the neighborhood crazy lady. She liked me a lot because I used to ask her opinion on things.

Leon raked up grass clippings and carried them around back to Billy's compost pile. Leon liked to work. He did odd jobs all around the neighborhood, but you had to keep your eye on him or he would work too hard. We put the tools away and went to my house.

My mother came in while we were drinking iced tea in the kitchen. She had another date with Robby, the used-car salesman, and was very excited. She said, "Can you eat at Billy's?"

"Yeah. I didn't get kicked out of school, Mom."

"I knew you wouldn't."

"Where you going?"

"Just out," she said from the bathroom. "Robby said it was a surprise and I don't know what to wear."

Leon pleaded with Billy and me to come to his house for supper, so we let him talk us into it. His mother was a great cook and his great-grandmother told marvelous stories. We told him we would come and he put on his cap and left.

Billy said, "The funeral is Sunday."

"Holder's funeral?"

"Yes. Know what I'm thinking of doing?"

I shook my head, sipping iced tea.

Before Billy could answer, Mom came into the kitchen. She had a hanger with white slacks and a red blouse. She said, "What do you think, honey?"

I said, "Wear the blue blouse. Goes better with your eyes."

"You're right. I'll wear the blue one."

She flitted out of the kitchen. I asked Billy, "What are you thinking of doing?"

"Searching Holder's house while his wife is gone."

"What for?"

Billy shrugged his shoulders. "I don't know. Just look around, see if I can find anything."

"Cocaine? Counterfeit hundreds? Hand grenades? What?"

"Just anything. I figure the more we know about Holder, the better. Like Mote says, knowing is always better than not knowing."

Mom came back into the kitchen, wearing her white slacks

and blue blouse. She walked back and forth, doing modeling turns and struck a couple of poses. "How do I look?"

"Terrific," I said. "Like the homecoming queen."

She gave me a kiss on the forehead and walked out, clicking her high heels and taking short steps the way she did when she was excited.

I looked at Billy. "Do you think there's any chance that Mote killed Holder?"

"Nope."

"Me neither. But it does look bad, doesn't it? His knife and the way he's disappeared. If I was a policeman, I would think that Mote was the killer."

Billy said, "That's why we have to find out who did it."

▲ *4* ▲

BILLY KNOCKED on the front door and Leon's sister opened it and smiled. Willa was sixteen and wonderfully put together. No matter how often I saw her, I was shocked by her figure each time. She was wearing tight red shorts and we followed her into the kitchen. I could tell that she knew I was watching her by the way she walked. Willa enjoyed being looked at, which meant that we were both having a good time.

Leon's father, Sampson, was reading the newspaper in their living room. He looked up and said, "There's my boys."

When we first started hanging out with Leon, Sampson used to call Billy and me "the twins." It was some kind of joke he made because he said he couldn't tell us apart, because all white folks looked alike. Later he called us "my boys," and I liked it better.

The first time I met Sampson was at our clubhouse. Billy and I were going to spend the night there and had invited Leon to join us. It was shortly after Mote had left that first summer. Leon went home to ask permission and came back with his dad. Sampson was a huge man, over six feet tall and probably two hundred eighty pounds. He would have looked great at two forty. He shook our hands and asked a few questions. He had pale blue eyes and noticed that I was staring at them.

"You don't see many blue-eyed niggers, do you, Chris?"

24

I said, "No, sir. You sure don't."

Leon and his great-grandmother, Ozzie, were already seated at the table. Ozzie patted the chairs on either side of her seat when she saw Billy and me, and we sat down after hugging her frail shoulders. Sampson and his wife, Rosie, were putting steaming bowls of food on the table. There were green beans, baked potatoes, broccoli, corn bread, and a large tossed salad.

Rosie said, "Leon says he fixed your lawn mower for you."

"Yes, ma'am," I said. "He sure did."

Sampson asked about the Holder affair and Billy told him everything we knew. Leon was watching me with his eyebrows raised and I opened my mouth and showed him my half-chewed food. He got excited and started to giggle. His mother scolded him with one word: "Leon!" Leon couldn't think fast enough to tell on me, and even if he had, Rosie wouldn't have believed him. She thought I was a "nice boy" because of the way I acted around her.

Ozzie went at her food slowly and deliberately, taking small bites. Her wrists and fingers were misshapen and knotted with arthritis. She weighed about eighty-five pounds and when I asked her how old she was she said, "Scarin' ninety to death."

I said, "Wasn't Mrs. Holder real active in your church, Ozzie?"

"Hmp," Ozzie said. "She prays on the bus."

I felt like I knew all I needed to know about Mrs. Holder's religious convictions. One time I asked Ozzie, "How come you celebrate Christmas if you're a Jehovah's Witness?"

Ozzie said, " 'Cause I really likes it."

Sampson said, "How come you boys are so certain that Mote didn't kill Holder?"

Billy said, "You just have to know Mote. You know him, Leon. Do you think Mote could kill anybody?"

Leon said, "Mote is a nice man, but Holder was a bad man." Leon frowned and breathed hard through his nose.

"Did you have some trouble with Mr. Holder?" I asked.

"Pass me some broccoli, Chris," Sampson said. I looked at

him and he shook his head no and glanced at Leon. Leon was acting nervous, jabbing around at his food with his fork.

We talked about other things as we finished the meal. Sampson asked about the city tennis tournament and I told him the finals were tomorrow. "Is it okay if Leon comes?" I asked. "I always play better when Leon's there to coach me."

"Yeah, it's all right," Sampson said.

After supper Leon, Billy, Willa, Ozzie, and I moved to the front porch. I got Ozzie a can of beer and she closed her eyes and sipped and rocked for a few minutes. No one spoke. She took another sip and rocked some more, keeping time to some internal rhythm. When she got her rocking chair going just right she said, "I want to tell you boys about Jim."

Leon was looking at me again. I stuck my tongue out at him.

"One day I ast him, 'What's the rest of your name besides Jim?' He looked at me real funny and said, 'Jim was all they ever told me.' "

A few more rocks. "He had seven dogs and chewed tobacco and liked to get water from our well. He came every day, morning and night, for his water and brought all his dogs, and we children was so afraid that his tobacco juice would seep down into our well water."

She took another sip from the can. "After he drank his water he would tell a joke. It was the same joke every day and when he finished he would turn to one of his dogs and say, 'Ain't that right?' and the leastest dog would bark.

"My sister say, 'Jim, how come your other dogs ain't trained and he only got one trick?'

"Jim say, 'They all trained and they all got their tricks, but this here's my special dog. He's the only one I let sleep with his head on my pillow.' "

Ozzie was off and running. "And them dogs were smart. They could . . . they knew how to line up. Jim would say, 'Okay, you all get together now,' and they would get in a row with the leastest dog, Tippy, in front of them. They would sit up with their little hands like this." Ozzie held her hands up by her chest.

I looked around at the others. They were all smiling. When I looked at Willa she smiled and dropped her head.

"Jim say, 'How do a dead dog look?' and those dogs would lie down on their sides, wagging their tails. Jim say, 'Dead dogs don't wag their tails,' and they'd stop."

Ozzie's eyes shone with old memories. She rocked over a loose board on the porch floor. It tapped out a slow, steady beat that matched the cadence of her words.

"One day there was a knock on the door and my sister get it. She came back in the kitchen and say, 'You won't believe it. Jim's married and she's here with Jim and all his dogs.'

"We went to the living room and Jim say, 'This here's my wife, Eve Mae Taylor. Eve, these here is my nigger friends.'

"Mama say, 'Well, Jim, now we know your last name.'

"Jim say, 'No, missie. I'm still just Jim. When we went for our license and they take our blood, they ask me what's my last name and I told them all I had was Jim. So they ask who the people I worked for's name, and I say Taylor. We on our way to town to get a bed and a mirror, so she can see comb her hair. And a plate for Eve. I only got eight plates.' "

Ozzie rocked some more. She tipped back the last of her beer and laid down the can. "Next time I tell you about my grandma," Ozzie said. "She used to get us all together like this on the porch and tell us stories about slavin' days."

I would have liked to hear another story but knew better than to ask. Ozzie always told us a story when we visited. She never told two. She drank only one beer every night too. Ozzie knew her limits.

Billy and I stood to leave. We gave Ozzie hugs and I straightened Leon's glasses and told him I would see him in the morning. Willa stood up. I wanted to hug Willa and I think she wanted to hug me back. I shook her hand instead.

As we walked home I replayed Ozzie's story in my mind. Billy must have been doing the same thing. As we crossed Woodlawn Avenue he said, " 'I only got eight plates.' "

I said, "Yeah, wasn't that great?"

▲ 5 ▲

LEON TOOK his coaching job seriously. He was dressed in tennis shorts, shoes, and shirt, with sweatbands on his forehead and each wrist. He put extra towels, adhesive tape, and a Thermos in the backseat and I backed his car out of the garage.

Leon buckled his seat belt. "Who we playing, Chris?"

"Crayton. Miles Crayton."

"He any good?"

"He's great, Leon. He's a left-hander and plays like John McEnroe. I'm going to need all the help you can give me."

"Play hard," Leon said. "Play hard, grit your teeth, and don't never give up."

"I don't know, Leon. I was thinking of playing real easy, missing shots, and falling down a lot."

Leon said, "No, Chris. Play hard and don't fall down."

"You think so?"

"Yeah, you listen what I tell you."

"Okay, Coach." We turned onto Central Avenue. "You remember all the signals, Leon?"

"Uh-huh. I studied them last night."

Leon and I had worked out a lot of hand signals that he was supposed to use during my matches. Holding up a fist meant Hit the ball harder. Making circular motions with his head meant Hit the ball higher. Running in place meant Move faster. We probably had about fifty signals and Leon knew them all. At least I think he knew them all. I had forgotten most of them, but every time I looked over at Leon during a match he would be standing up and signaling like crazy. People would look at him.

There was a terrible smell in the car and I rolled down my window. "Leon, did you pass gas?"

"What?"

"Did you pass gas?"

"Huh?"

"Leon, did you fart?"

"No. I didn't fart, Chris. Really."

"Well, roll down your window." Leon had the worst gas in the world. It did something to the back of my nose that made me angry. I said, "Leon, it's okay to fart. Everybody does that. It's a normal thing, but when you're in the car it's best to roll down the window first."

We pulled into the tennis-court complex and found a parking slot. Leon carried my rackets, gym bag, his towels, tape, and Thermos into the locker room and put them by my locker. We could hear the cheers and applause from a match that was in progress on center court. I told Leon to go find out what the score was.

Leon went out and I took off my pants and shoes. Leon came back and stood in the doorway with his chin on his chest. He was working his jaw muscles. "Hey, Chris," he said, not looking up. "I'm sorry I farted."

"It's all right, Leon. Go find out the score."

Another cheer went up from the grandstand and I was glad that there was a big crowd. I always played better with a lot of people watching, especially if there were girls.

I dressed in brand-new clothes from the skin out, a luxury I saved for tournament finals. I checked myself out in the mirror. The clothes looked good, but I looked the same—too skinny, especially in the neck, the forehead slanted too much, and the ears were wrong too.

Coach Sherman came into the dressing room. He was wearing black trousers, a checked jacket, light blue shirt, yellow tie, polished low-cut boots, and a pink show hankie in his jacket pocket. Mr. Sherman was an assistant football coach and knew nothing about tennis. He accompanied the tennis team on road trips and hung around tournaments I played in, hoping to get his picture taken.

He said, "How you feel, Chris?"

"I feel fine, Coach."

"Feeling good?"

"Yeah."

"Huh?"

"I feel good."

"Huh?"

"Feel real good."

"Feeling good, huh?"

"Yeah, I feel good."

Mr. Sherman picked up one of my rackets and scratched his back with it. "That creepy guy's out there. What's his name?"

"Leon."

"Yeah, Leon. That creepy guy. He's out there."

"He came with me, Coach."

"He's kinda creepy, ain't he?"

"No, he's okay. Just a little retarded."

"Gives me the creeps, you know?"

"Those are great threads, Coach."

"Hey, thanks." Mr. Sherman went over to the mirror and fooled with the knot on his yellow tie. "Not bad, huh?"

"Not bad," I said. "Looking good."

He tugged at his jacket and thumbed the lapels. "You like the coat?"

"Sharp, Coach."

"Huh?"

"Sharp jacket."

"How you feel?"

"I'm fine, Coach. I feel good."

"You ain't nervous, are you?"

"Just a little. It's okay, Coach. I play better when I'm a little nervous. I'll settle down once the match starts."

"Not too nervous?"

"No. Just a little excited."

"Take a good shit?"

"Yeah, I did that at home."

"Good shit? Get it all out?"

"Yeah, it was fine."

"Need to shit some more?"

"No."

"You need to shit, you got time."

"I don't need to."

"Huh?"

"I don't need to shit."

I pulled on a pair of cotton warm-up pants. Coach Sherman walked over to the urinal and spit. "Got a jockstrap on, Chris?"

"Sure."

"Good jockstrap?"

"Yeah, It's brand-new."

"Huh?"

"I've got on a good jockstrap."

"Good and firm?"

"Uh-huh."

"Good firm jock?"

"Yeah, Coach. It's a great jockstrap."

"Nuts ain't hanging out the side?"

"No."

"Huh?"

"Nuts are fine."

"Nuts hang out the side, you can't run."

I got out three rackets and began roughing up the handles with a piece of sandpaper. "How about you, Coach? You okay?"

"Yeah, fine."

"Huh?"

"I'm fine."

"Huh?"

"Don't do that, Chris. Don't talk like that."

"Huh?"

"Don't . . . Come on, cut it out. Jesus, you're weird sometimes. You know that? You're really weird sometimes."

I stood up quickly and gave Mr. Sherman a kiss on the
cheek. He said, "Hey, man," and pulled out his handkerchief
and wiped his cheek. "Don't fool around like that. Know
what I mean?"

"It's that pink handkerchief, Coach."

"Huh?"

"That pink hankie."

"It look queer?"

"Yeah."

"Looks queer, huh?"

"Looks queer, Coach."

Mr. Sherman put his handkerchief in his hip pocket as we
walked outside. The women's finals were being played on the
center court. It was three games each in the final set. We
watched them play a point. Both girls stood deep behind the
baseline and hit blooper balls back and forth. Boring tennis.

Mr. Sherman said, "Too bad about Holder, huh?"

"Yeah."

"I mean, he's dead, right?"

"Right."

"Dead as a hammer."

"I'm going to warm up, Coach. See you later."

Miles Crayton was practicing serves on a back court, big
sweeping serves with lots of topspin. He pretended that he
didn't see me coming and hit a few real boomers, ticking the
side of the lines and raising chalk dust.

I walked up to the net and laid down my rackets. Miles
said, "Hey, Chris."

"Hi, Miles."

We began warming up together, hitting lazy forehands
and backhands. Miles was an experienced tournament player
too and we didn't try any psychological tricks on each other.
We both knew each other's game from four previous matches.
I had won three and they were each very close, hard-fought
battles.

The umpire announced, "Five games to three, third set," and we began hitting a little harder. Miles came to net and pointed up, signaling that he wanted to practice some overhead smashes. I hit him some lobs and Miles put them away crisply. He had a fine overhead game and I made myself stop admiring it.

More cheering from the women's match. I was hitting well, seeing the ball clearly and enjoying it. Tennis had come easy for me and I had worked hard to improve my game. It was really the only thing I had ever worked hard at.

Mote had watched me win the public-parks tournament last September. We put the trophy on a shelf in the shack. Mote said, "I learned something about you today, Chris."

I said, "What's that?"

Mote adjusted the trophy, moving it an inch to the left. "Well, first of all, you are great fun to watch. You'd be worth paying to see."

"Thanks, Mote."

He sat down. "But what really surprised me was how much you enjoyed breaking the other kid's spirit."

"What do you mean?"

"You know what I mean. You crushed him." He smiled at me. "In fact, it bordered on cruelty. I felt sorry for him."

"Really. You think he'll get over it?"

"Sure. He's young. Give him a couple of days to think about it and he'll probably get mad, decide to practice harder to get back at you. Beat you next time."

"Never," I said. "He knows he'll never beat me. Deep down, he knows."

Mote nodded his head. "Exactly. Like I said, you crushed him."

We walked down the bank to Mote's camp. He lit a fire and put on his coffeepot. I said, "One time I was playing this guy from St. Mary's. It was a school match on his school's courts and all his friends were there. I won the first set and was ahead three to one in the second. All I had to do was run out three more games, and then it happened." I snapped my fingers.

Mote added some sticks to the fire. "What happened?"

"I just . . . I got to thinking about how he was feeling. He was a real nice guy and I started to think how he must be feeling, with all his friends there and everything. I sort of eased up on him. I thought I'd just let him win a game or two. And the next thing you know, he won the set. I tried to pick it back up, but I just couldn't and he beat me in the final set."

Mote said, "So now you go for the throat, huh?"

"Yeah. I mean, I've got to. Sometimes I start feeling sorry for the guy I play and I have to get off that real quick, find some reason to be mad at him."

"How about the cruel part? Do you enjoy that?"

I said, "I didn't think anyone knew about that. I thought it was my secret."

"Do you enjoy it?"

"Yeah, Mote. I sure do. You think that's wrong?"

"No, I don't think so. Not as long as you own up to it." He smiled at me and poured our coffee. "Just watch it— make sure you leave it on the court."

Miles and I started hitting harder. He was a banger. When he got in his groove he could hit the ball as hard as anyone I ever played. He looked a lot better warming up than I did.

"Game to Miss Forbes. Miss Reynolds leads five games to four." Miles hit a forehand crosscourt like a bullet. I said, "Better save those, Miles."

Miles grinned and hit another one even harder. "I got plenty," he said.

I missed two backhands in a row, catching the top of the net. "Backhand looks shaky," Miles said. I missed another, then another, and Miles laughed.

A big cheer. The umpire announced, "Game, set, and match to Miss Reynolds. She wins six–three, five–seven, six–four. The boys' finals will start in ten minutes."

Miles and I gathered up our rackets. He said, "I hear you been beating up on a teacher."

"Yeah," I said. "He made fun of my backhand. I don't take that from anybody."

"Who is the guy that killed him?" Miles asked. "Mo?"

"Mote. The police think that Mote killed him, but he didn't do it."

"Probably on your mind," Miles said. "Probably hurt your concentration."

I smiled at him. "You're a prick, Miles."

"I know."

We walked to the court together. Leon was in his seat directly behind the umpire's chair, glaring at Miles. Leon hated all my opponents.

Miles won the toss for serve. I took the east court and we continued our warm-up. The spectators were returning to the stands and Miles's big crushing drives drew a few "Oohs" and "Aahs" from the crowd. Most people, watching us warm up, would figure that Miles was a much better player. We hit some practice serves as the umpire introduced us. There was polite applause, with Leon's voice cutting through with "Come on, Chris."

Miles won the first game easily on four straight points. When we changed sides Leon handed me some water. I said, "This guy's great, Leon. Too good for me. Why don't I just give up and we'll take in a movie?"

"No, Chris. Listen, hit straight balls he can't reach."

"Straight balls, huh?"

"Uh-huh. And down the sides."

"I'll give it a try, Leon. Thanks."

I spun my first serve in wide to Miles's backhand and came to the net. Miles hit it crosscourt and I was waiting there to block it back into the open court for a winner. I looked over at Leon and winked. Leon was giving me some signal that I didn't recognize. On the next point I hit a clean winner off my backhand, getting my shoulder into it. It's one of the best feelings in the world.

I got a ball from the ball boy and saw Mote standing by the side of the grandstand. Our eyes locked for just a second, then I glanced away. I missed a routine backhand and made a slow process of untying and retying my shoelaces, trying to get my mind back on the match.

I held serve and so did Miles. We sat down and toweled off after the third game. Leon said, "You can do it, Chris."

I said, "Leon, after the match I want you to tell me about the trouble you had with Mr. Holder."

"I didn't, Chris. I didn't have no trouble."

"Don't lie to me, Leon. I've got to know. It will be between you and me."

We each held serve until four games all. It was a good match and the crowd was into it. I was playing for a cute brunette in the third row. With Miles serving at four games–all and thirty–all, he hit a lob over my head that I had to scramble back for. It didn't look like I could get to the ball, but I chased it down and smacked it with a between-the-legs shot that was perfect, sailing past the lunging Miles and landing one inch inside the sideline. The crowd stood and cheered and Miles's shoulders seemed to sag a bit. On the next point I was still pumped up from the cheering and pasted a crosscourt forehand to win the game. We sat down by the umpire's chair.

Leon said, "Chris, I didn't lie to you, man. I don't know nothin' about Mr. Holder."

"Remember how bad you felt when you lied to me about the fart in the car, Leon?"

"Ah, Chris. It wasn't nothin'."

I wiped off the handle of my racket. "I've got to win this game, Leon. Any suggestions?"

"Nah."

"Come on, Leon. Hang in there with me."

"It wasn't nothin', Chris. Just a paper Mr. Holder had."

"A paper?"

"Uh-huh. Some paper he had people to sign."

I stood up and drank some water. "Thanks for telling me, Leon. After the match we'll talk it over. Right now I want to break this guy's heart."

I had been serving to Miles's backhand during the entire match and figured that he would be expecting it again. I hit my first serve down the center line for an ace and felt him weaken just a bit. I served out the game and won the first set. The brunette was looking at me. It was a I-think-you're-wonderful look, but I acted like I didn't see it.

Miles pulled himself together and served a strong game to go up one to nothing in the second set. At the court change I said, "Leon, I've got to get this off my mind. What kind of paper?"

Leon was breathing hard through his nose. "Some paper," he said. "Some paper that said I should be put away in some kind of home for folks that are mental. Had people sign it."

"How did you find out about it, Leon?"

"Somebody tell Willa." Leon was close to crying.

"Leon, look, you told me and it's all over and you're my pal and my coach. Let's beat this asshole and go home."

"Play hard, Chris."

I put on a new wristband. "Should I hit straight balls?"

Leon wiped his eyes. "Yeah, and down the sides."

I held serve and glanced at the brunette. Detective Stienert was sitting behind her. I wondered if he had come to see me or was looking for Mote. Either way, it bothered me to see him there and I missed some routine shots.

Miles took advantage of my letdown, raised the level of his play, and won three games in a row. Leon was going crazy, using every signal he could think of. At four games to one I looked over at him and he was standing on one leg and flapping his elbows like a chicken. Good old Leon.

During the next game Miles got a bad call and began protesting and pouting the way McEnroe does. I went over to the stands to Detective Stienert and said, "What's up?"

"Just come to watch you play," he said.

"Anything new on the case?"

"Nope, nothing new." He leaned closer. "This boy going to whip your butt if you don't start playing."

I reached over and touched his moon scar. "That's for

luck," I said. The brunette was taking it all in. She had a slight overbite, just enough.

Stienert said, "You supposed to rub my head."

Miles was still arguing. I said, "Come on, Miles. Let's play. You've been studying those old McEnroe tapes too much."

There was laughter from the crowd and some applause. Miles double-faulted and missed a forehand. I felt a comeback coming on, broke his serve, and held my own to pull within one game, four–three. We sat down between games.

Leon was all worked up. "You can do it, Chris. I know you can."

I said, "I don't know, Leon." I took a sip of water. "What do you say I just quit, Leon? Give up. Then we could go play some putt-putt golf, get a Dairy Queen."

"Don't say that."

I took another drink of water and looked around. Mote was sitting on the far side of the grandstand. The TV-news cameras were being set up on the other side of the court. As I stood up Miles passed and said, "Getting tired?"

I walked to my side of the court, staying near the stands. When I passed the brunette I said, "Are you married or engaged or anything?"

She shook her head no. I think my face flushed red. Probably from all the heat and exertion.

Miles had his power game working and was running me from side to side on every point. The cameramen were getting good film for the evening news and at one point Miles dove for a ball, stretching out at full extension to slap a forehand down the line for a clean winner. It was a wonderful shot. The crowd cheered and I dropped my racket and applauded along with them. Leon was booing at Miles through cupped hands.

We played to six games each and Miles served first in the tiebreaker. I didn't want to play a third set. Miles had run me hard and I was getting leg-weary. It had been three nights since Holder's murder and I hadn't slept well. Miles served an ace, kicking up chalk as the ball ticked the line.

The linesman called, "Out," and the crowd whistled and booed. Miles went into a tantrum and I sat down by Leon while he argued. Leon said, "He's a sorehead, Chris. He's a bad sport."

"That was a bad call, Leon. I don't blame him."

"It was out, Chris."

"No, it wasn't. It was in. I'm going to lose the point on purpose."

Miles was still fussing with the umpire. I walked over to the brunette. "Could I call you sometime?"

She said, "Yes." I love it when they say yes.

I asked Detective Stienert if he had a pen. He handed me a pen and a piece of paper. "Way to go, Little Moon."

Her name was Vicki Long. She made little circles over the *i*'s, but I liked her anyway. With an overbite, you can get away with that kind of stuff. I put the paper in my gym bag and listened to the umpire give Miles a ten-second warning. We took our positions and the umpire said, "Second serve."

Miles hit his serve and I caught the ball in my left hand, conceding the point. The crowd loved it and gave me a big hand. Vicki really thought I was wonderful now, but Miles didn't. He knew I was hot-dogging, showing off with a cheap gesture that made him look like a nerd. Several people yelled "Let's go, Chris," and the umpire had to ask for silence.

I served to his forehand and came to net. Miles chipped a return down the line. The backhand side of his court was open and he moved toward his right. I volleyed behind him, wrong-footing him, and he fell down hard, trying to change directions. I grabbed a towel and ran over to his side of the court in a pretended concern for possible injury. "You looked silly as hell on that one, Miles."

Miles took the towel and brushed clay from his legs.

I said, "Probably hurt your concentration, a dumb-looking fall like that."

"You're a prick, Chris," he said.

"I know."

He picked up his racket and handed me the towel. I wiped clay from the back of his shirt and said, "Isn't this nice of me, doing this for you?"

I won the tiebreaker, the set, and the match. Vicki put two fingers in her mouth and whistled over the sound of applause. I liked that a lot. Leon pounded my back a little too hard.

After the awards ceremony I showered and changed while Leon held my trophy, rubbing his big hands over it. He looked all worn out. I think my matches took more out of Leon than they took out of me. There was a lot of backslapping in the locker room from people I didn't know. In the shower Miles said, "I would have beaten you in the third set."

He was probably right. I said, "Never."

Leon held my trophy and grinned on the way out of the parking lot. I asked him who else knew about Holder's paper and he said, "Nobody. Just Mom, Dad, Willa, and you."

"The people who signed it would know, Leon."

Leon rolled down his window and farted. He smiled over at me and I said, "That's good, Leon."

▲ 6 ▲

BILLY AND I were in the backyard of a house across the street from the Holder place at ten o'clock, lying under some kind of sweet-smelling bushes. At eleven-thirty Mrs. Holder came out of the front door. Mr. Douglas was with her.

Billy said, "You think he spent the night?"

"I don't know."

They walked to a car parked on the street. Mr. Douglas held the door open for Mrs. Holder and walked around to the driver's side. He looked up and down the street before he got in and drove off.

"How we going to get in, Billy?"

"Around back," he said. "Let's go."

We walked across the street and around to the back of the house. Billy went up to some French doors and laid down his sack. He took out a small plunger and pushed it against a pane. Then he got out a can of glazing compound and pulled a jackknife from his pocket. "We'll take the glaze off this window, reach in, and open the door." He carved a piece of the white glaze off and put it in his sack. "Saw it on *Rockford*. While I reglaze the window you can start searching the house."

"By myself?"

Billy worked on the window. I walked up to the back door and tried it. It was locked. I looked under the mat and saw a key. "*Psst,* Billy." I held up the key. Billy put his knife away,

41

pulled the plunger loose, and put everything back in the sack. I unlocked the door and put the key back under the mat. We looked at each other a moment, then went in.

Billy laid his sack on the kitchen table and we listened to empty-house sounds. My pulse rate went to about two hundred. The house smelled like *I shouldn't be here* and burnt toast. Whole wheat. Billy said, "You start upstairs, I'll check the basement."

I walked up the stairs. There were two bedrooms and a bath and I went into the bedroom with the unmade bed. *What if they forgot something and came back?* I looked in the top drawer of a dresser. It was full of black socks tucked into little balls. I wondered what she would do with them, now that Mr. Holder wouldn't be needing them. The second drawer had underwear, Jockey shorts, and sleeveless undershirts. The third drawer had sweatshirts in it and the bottom drawer was full of *National Geographic* magazines. Pretty suspicious stuff.

The other dresser held Mrs. Holder's things. I looked in the closet. Men's stuff on the right, women's on the left. I pulled over a chair and stood on it to look at the top shelf. There were some blankets, pillow slips, a straw hat, and a .22 pistol. I smelled the pistol, just like a real detective. It smelled oily.

There were no dead bodies under the bed. I skipped the bathroom and went into the other bedroom and didn't find anything unusual. There was a trapdoor in the back wall of the closet and I pushed it open. It was a storage area, with a metal Christmas tree, some ornaments, an electric toaster, a hat box, and some cobwebs. I shook the hat box and it was empty.

I started downstairs and heard a noise. Someone turned the front doorknob. I heard the door open and a few whispered words.

Footsteps. I backed up the stairs and tiptoed to the second bedroom. Voices from the first floor were muffled. I went into the closet, crawled through the trapdoor, and closed it behind me. I was directly over the voices.

One voice said, "Maybe it's in here."

Another voice said, "Take it all."

Drawers opened and closed. If they were quiet, they could hear my heartbeat and find me. A voice said, "Let's go."

Footsteps. The front door shut. Then silence. Car doors slammed, an engine started. I discovered that I had my eyes squeezed tightly shut, so they couldn't see me, I guess. I breathed through my mouth and listened to the silence. I listened so hard that it made my joints ache.

I crept back down the stairs and nosed around in the kitchen. In the living room there was a bookcase filled with romance novels. The covers all showed some woman in a long dress, either running away from a spooky-looking castle or being swept up in some guy's arms. The carpet had been taken up and in the middle of the room an area of the subfloor had been sanded.

There was a room off the living room that must have been Holder's den. In the second drawer of his desk I found a lot of poorly printed pamphlets devoted to hating blacks and Jews. I glanced through them quickly. "Martin Luther Coon, Public Enemy Number One." Another was about "Jesse Jackass." The Holders had refined literary tastes. I looked through the other drawers and they were empty, except for a few paper clips, some rubber bands, stamps, envelopes, and paper. Whoever had been downstairs had cleaned out the desk. I heard Billy climbing the steps and went into the hallway. He held up a metal box and said, "I got it. Let's go."

We left by the front door. I wanted to run, but we made ourselves walk with exaggerated casualness. Any more casual and we would have fallen down. Billy said, "Holder had a printing shop in his basement."

"A printing shop?"

"Uh-huh. It looked like professional-quality equipment. There was a big press and a small one, some paper cutters, a copier, one of those light tables with a camera mounted over it."

We crossed the street. I told Billy about all the pamphlets I had found. "I'll bet Holder printed that stuff."

Billy said, "He did a lot of printing for school too. There were some exams, football schedules, newsletters from the drama club."

We walked another half block before Billy stopped suddenly. "I left the sack," he said. "I left the sack with my stuff in it on the kitchen table." We turned around and looked back, then we took off and ran the last four blocks to our clubhouse.

"We're going to have to remember to buy a new lock," Billy said. There were bright scratches on the metal door latch where the detectives had pried off the lock.

Billy handed me the box and collapsed on the cot. It was a small metal box, the kind that would hold a hundred index cards. I opened the lid and took out photographs. The first photograph showed Mrs. Holder getting into a Volkswagen beetle. There was some kind of store in the background and I couldn't see the driver. The next picture showed the VW in front of a motel. A man was walking into the office. The next picture was of Mrs. Holder and the man entering a room. It had been taken with a long-range lens and had that wavy look. The man had his back to the camera. The fourth picture was taken through some window blinds and was out of focus. I couldn't make anything out. The fifth one was taken after dark. It showed two people leaving the motel room, silhouetted in the doorway from the light inside the room.

"Hanky-panky," I said.

Billy said, "Uh-huh."

"Where were these?"

Billy sat up. "You know the little door in a water heater? Where you open it to light it. It was in there."

"What made you look in there?"

"I don't know. I just looked everywhere. What do you think we should do?"

"I don't know. We could give these to the police."

"It's called breaking and entering, Chris."

"We could mail them," I said. "Just put them in an envelope and mail them to Baker. Maybe a note saying that this is Holder's wife."

Billy said, "I wish we could tell who that man is."

I went through the pictures again. "Hey, Billy. On this one you can almost make out the license plate."

Billy looked at it. "If you could enlarge it."

"Uh-huh."

We went to my house to get a magnifying glass. Mom was sitting in the kitchen, drinking orange juice and reading the paper. She had on a ratty dressing gown, bunny slippers, and hair curlers. She was still beautiful. She smiled when we came in, a real dazzler of a smile that looked the way bells sound in the distance. "I was just reading about my famous son," she said.

I gave Mom a hug and looked at the sports page over her shoulder. There were two pictures from the match. One was a very good picture of me hitting a forehand. It showed the ball flattened against the strings and I was looking right at it, the way you're supposed to. The other picture showed me wiping off Miles's back after his fall. Under the picture it said Good Sportsmanship.

"Where's your trophy?" Mom said. "I looked in your room."

"It's at Leon's. I told him he could keep it for a while."

"Oh, Chris"—she stuck out her lower lip—"your father will want to see it."

"Is he coming over?"

"Uh-huh. Later tonight, about six or so. I thought we could have supper. He's very proud of you, you know. So am I."

I said, "Aw, shucks."

Billy got two apples from the refrigerator and handed me one. Mom reached into her dressing gown and pulled out a slip of paper. "You've got some phone calls," she said. "Mr. Sweeny, from Cassidy University. He sounded real nice. He wants to talk to you about a tennis scholarship. And somebody named Moon. He left a number."

I said, "How was your date?"

"Good. We had a wonderful time."

"You like this guy a lot, don't you?"

"Yes, I do. I want you to meet him. He wants to meet you too. I know you'll like him."

I knew that I wouldn't like him. I never liked any of Mom's boyfriends. Usually I didn't say anything, but a couple of times I had to talk her out of going out with guys she brought around. Mom could pick some real losers.

One good thing about Mom, she would take my advice on things like that. Over the last two years our relationship had gradually changed, and sometimes I was more like the parent than she was. It was a pretty good arrangement.

Billy and I went into my room. We looked at the pictures through the magnifying glass, but it didn't help. We got into our conference positions. He lay on the lower bunk and I lay on the top bunk, hanging down over the side, looking at him upside down.

"Did you see who came in, Chris?"

"No, I was hiding. Whoever it was cleaned out Holder's desk."

"Were you scared?"

"I'm still scared."

"Me too."

Billy had his fingers laced behind his head. "We could confront Mrs. Holder," he said. "Show her the pictures, ask her about Mr. Douglas."

I said, "I think we should talk to Detective Stienert."

"And give him the pictures?"

"Uh-huh. I bet they could blow up the photograph and get the license number. Maybe track down the guy. He has to be a good suspect, screwing Holder's wife, Holder knowing about it."

"We don't know that, Chris. We don't know that they were screwing."

"Come on, Billy." I put my hands behind my back and did some reverse sit-ups, arching my back at the top of the swing. "You think they were holding a prayer meeting in the motel room?"

Billy smiled. I said, "That's just like you. Never believing people do anything wrong, always giving them the benefit of the doubt. You always do that."

"No, I don't."

"Sure you do. You think everyone is nice and honest and fair. You think everyone is like you. It's part of your charm. It's what makes you so lovable."

Mom knocked on the door and said, "Telephone."

I picked up the phone and Mote's voice said, "Chris?"

I said, "Hold on. Don't talk for just a minute." I put my hand over the mouthpiece and told Billy, "It's Mote. I'm going to pick up the hall phone."

Mom was watching a war movie on TV. John Wayne was killing the Japs. He got about fourteen while I walked though the room.

Mote wanted to know if we were ready for final exams. Billy said, "What happened, Mote?"

"Nothing. I mean, I went fishing, downstream to that big hole of water. I was coming back when I saw a car parked by the shack and two guys walking around. I could tell they were cops and I hid in the trees and watched them. After they left I packed my stuff and took off. I guess they think I killed Holder. I've been listening to the radio."

I said, "Where are you?"

"Remember that place I took you guys fishing last fall?"

"Yeah. You gonna stay there?"

"For a few days."

Billy said, "They think you did it, Mote. Holder was stabbed with one of your knives. The police are looking for you."

"I know. Chris, I want to congratulate you on the tennis championship. You played a fine match."

"Thanks," I said. "Mote, why did you run?"

Mote groaned again. "Kind of a long story, Chris. I just didn't want to go to jail. There's some things I never told you guys. I just don't think I could stand it, being locked up."

Billy said, "Does it have to do with Vietnam?"

"Yeah. You know about that, huh?"

I said, "The police told us, Mote. No details, just that you were a prisoner and were tortured. Is that why you never slept inside?"

I could hear Mote take a deep breath and let it out. "Yeah. I think I spent some time in a small space. A couple of months."

Billy said, "Think? Aren't you sure?"

"Can't remember," Mote said. "Not all of it."

No one spoke. I listened to background noise.

Mote said, "I better go. You boys be good. I'll call you in a few days."

I said, "Mote?"

"Yeah?"

"Uh, how about sticking around when this is over?"

"What for?"

"I don't know. It's . . . all this stuff. I mean, you're kind of important to me."

Billy said, "Me too."

Mote said, "You guys are important to me too. More than you know." He clicked off.

I called Detective Stienert's number and a woman told me he wasn't in. I left my name and number.

I walked back through the living room. A medic was cleaning out a wound on John Wayne's left shoulder. He poured some liquid on it that probably burned like crazy, but John Wayne didn't even wince.

▲ 7 ▲

MY FATHER showed up at six. I opened the front door for
him and he put his hands on my shoulders. We were eye to
eye. He said, "You've grown some more," and we embraced,
slapping each other's back so it wouldn't be too sissy. "City
champ again, eh?"

"Yeah."

"How about that?"

Mom came out of the kitchen. They held hands and smiled
at each other for a moment. I thought they were going to
kiss, but it didn't quite happen.

They sat down on the sofa. Dad unbuttoned his sport coat
and smoothed his tie. "So how have you been, Rachel?"

"Fine. We've been just fine, haven't we, Chris?"

"Yeah, we've been fine. How about you, Dad?"

"Oh, fine, doing just fine."

Dad looked around the room while Mom studied the back
of her hands. I said, "How's business?"

"Good. Business is good. Record year so far."

A dog barked somewhere and a motorcycle went by the
house, making that angry noise. I said, "Can I get you a
beer?"

Dad said he wanted a beer and Mom asked me to bring
her her glass of wine. I went into the kitchen and got a bottle
of beer from the refrigerator. I never could figure out why
they had these occasional get-togethers. No one seemed to

get any pleasure from them and after Dad left, Mom always cried.

I got one of the tall, thin glasses that Dad liked. I could hear Mom making small talk about her job. I poured another inch of wine into Mom's glass. Maybe if I got them real drunk . . . I thought. Maybe if they both got smashed, they would talk about what was going on between them and either get back together or leave each other alone. Anything was better than this.

Dad poured his beer down the center of the glass, raising a thick foam. He poured only one swallow at a time. "Have you started drinking beer yet, Chris?"

"No, sir. Well, not very often."

"Still in training?"

"No. I just don't like it the way you do. It makes me sleepy."

Dad nodded, poured another swallow, and drank it. "Your mother said that you were getting scholarship inquiries."

I said, "I've talked to some people is all, Dad. Some people from Ohio State, Dayton University, and a phone call from Cassidy. Mr. Sherman says I should be hearing from the University of Georgia. That's his alma mater."

Mom said, "Take the one closest to home, Chris."

Dad said, "Naw, take the best offer, make the best deal you can, son. You can get home on holidays no matter where you go."

"I can't believe he'll be going away to college," Mom said.

"Me, neither," Dad said. He took another swallow of beer. "When the reporters talk to you, Chris . . . like after the match when the reporters talk to you . . ."

"Uh-huh."

"You know, instead of talking about Leon, thanking him for his help, you might give me a plug. Mention the company."

"Yeah, okay."

"I can't understand why you mess around with Leon anyway."

"Leon's a good guy, Dad. He's a friend and he's always for me. He's always a hundred percent for me."

"Maybe so, but it doesn't look good, Chris. People notice who your friends are and it doesn't look good for you to be hanging around so much with a retarded black man."

Mom was watching me closely. When I looked at her she had that pleading look in her eyes, begging me not to argue with Dad.

Dad said, "You don't realize it, Chris, but the friends you make now will be important to you later on. You should be making friends with kids who will be more important than Leon."

He poured another swallow of beer and watched the foam climb up the side of the glass. "It's all a game, Chris. A game of who you know. Who you know is more important than what you know. Remember that."

"I will."

"Being buddies with a nobody like Leon won't ever do you any good. Mentioning him in the press is doing him a favor. People trade in favors, you know—you scratch my back and I'll scratch yours."

"Uh-huh."

"And it really doesn't do Leon any good to have his name in the papers. You're wasting a favor."

"It does him some good, Dad. It makes him feel good and he probably won't get many chances to make the press."

"Well, you're still wasting an opportunity. Next time mention me, me and the company."

The phone rang. "I'll try, Dad." I picked up the phone.

Detective Stienert said, "What's happening, Little Moon?"

I said, "I would like to see you. We've got some evidence."

"It Baker's case. He in charge."

I said, "Do you ever say *is*?"

"*Is?*"

"Yeah, like, it *is* Baker's case. He *is* in charge."

Stienert laughed. "It called soul."

"It called dumb. It called soul, you live in Harlem. Go to college, it called Uncle Remus."

Stienert laughed again. "What you got, Little Moon?"

"I've got some hot stuff, but I don't want to give it to Baker."

"Evidence or rumors or what?"

"Evidence," I said. "Something you can hold in your hand. It will make you look good down at headquarters."

Stienert was silent for a moment. "I come by in a little bit."

"Make it about eight. My father's here."

Stienert said, "Okay, I see you about eight. Give me time to brush up on my grammar, diagram some sentences."

I helped Mom put the food on the table while Dad called his office. He gave someone a lot of stern instructions in his I'm-the-boss voice.

As we ate dinner we discussed the weather and agreed it had been a mild winter and a warm spring and that we could use some rain and where have the years gone and it seemed like only yesterday. Dad asked me about the Holder affair and I told him the things he could have read in the newspaper, leaving out the information Billy and I had found.

Dad said, "Holder sure was a funny fellow. He worked for me for twelve years, but I never really got to know him." Dad buttered a piece of bread. Then he wiped the bread back and forth on his ear of corn, spreading the butter. Mom watched him with her mouth turned down.

I said, "Is that why you guys broke up? Because of the way Dad butters his corn?"

Mom looked down at her plate. Dad said, "No, it was other things." He gave me his look, like I had an asshole right between my eyes. I hated that look.

About half the kids I know have divorced parents, but it doesn't seem to bother them very much. At least they act like it doesn't bother them. I act like it doesn't bother me either.

Five years ago when my parents decided to get a divorce, Dad moved out of the house and took an apartment. In the night I would be awakened by a sudden awareness of his absence. His absence somehow was a presence, like a stranger had moved in. I would get out of bed and go down to the basement where his workshop was set up. I would sit on his stool and handle his tools. Then I would go back to bed.

It was a bad time. I knew that having your parents get a divorce wasn't a big deal, but I wasn't taking it very well. I had a lot of crazy feelings about it—anger, guilt, shame, self-pity, and fear all mixed up together. The worst was the guilt. I would feel scared and guilty and didn't know why.

Then Mote showed up. Mote talked about things I had never heard anyone else talk about, things that mattered. He was always honest. One September Billy and I had walked up the creek to gather wood for Mote's campfire. Billy was telling me about a girl he was madly in love with.

I said, "Why don't you ask her out?"

Billy said, "Do you think she'd go?"

"I don't know." We picked up some more sticks and started back toward camp with armloads.

Billy said, "I think she likes me."

"How can you tell?"

"Well, when I say something that's funny she kind of leans toward me as she laughs and crinkles up her nose."

We dropped our sticks by the campfire. Mote started breaking them. I said, "That's a good sign. She probably does like you. She's probably sitting by the phone right now, waiting for you to call, leaning forward with her nose crinkled up."

"I tried to call her yesterday," Billy said. "Once I even dialed the number and when she picked up the phone, I hung up."

"Why did you hang up?"

Billy shrugged his shoulders. "I just did."

Mote said, "Being a teenager is the pits, isn't it?"

Billy said, "What do you mean, Mote?"

"I was just remembering, listening to you guys talk, remembering when I was your age and how miserable I was most of the time."

Billy said, "You were miserable?"

I got a drink of ice water from a Thermos. This was

interesting. Grown-ups had always told me what a paradise the teen years were. "These are the best years of your life," they would say.

Mote said, "Yeah, I sure was. Tough years—half man, half boy. All those sexual feelings, all the worries about whether people liked me. Wanting to be independent, but still knowing I was dependent on my parents. Very confusing."

I handed Billy the Thermos. "You went through all that stuff, Mote?"

"Sure I did."

"How long did it last?"

"I don't know. Hell, maybe I'm still going through it. I'm not sure we ever really grow up. Not all the way."

Mote seemed like the most grown-up person I had ever known. I said, "What do you mean?"

Mote stood and slapped at the seat of his pants. "Kind of hard to talk about, this kind of thing. Even hard to think about sometimes. You have to look at yourself and see things that aren't very pretty. It's hard work."

Billy said, "You can tell us, Mote. You can talk to us."

"I remember one thing that really tore me up when I was a kid." Mote turned over a five-gallon plastic pail and sat down on it. "I was about your age, Chris, and my parents had just gotten divorced. And you know what?"

"What?"

"Well, I was sad about it. You know, I missed having my dad around and felt sorry for myself, but I was glad about it at the same time."

"Why, Mote?" I said.

"Because," he said. "Now I had Mom all to myself. I didn't have Dad around to compete with all the time." Mote chuckled. "Really had me mixed up. Took me a long time to finally figure it out. Years."

Billy looked at me. "Do you ever feel that way, Chris?"

I said, "No." It *was* the way I felt. It was exactly the way I felt, but I said no.

Billy said, "You know what I do, Mote? Something I do, I

use the fact that my dad is dead to get pity. It's like, Poor little Billy, doesn't have a daddy."

Mote smiled. "Does it work?"

"Uh-huh, sometimes. I mean, it works on Grandma. She bakes me special cakes and stuff. Gives me things, presents. It works on other people too. I do it too much though. I shouldn't do it at all."

Mote said, "Is that the worst thing you've ever done?"

Billy waited a moment. "Yeah, I think it is."

Mote shook his head. "What a terrible person."

Billy laughed. I picked up some sticks and began breaking them across my leg.

That night I lay in bed and thought about the things Mote had said. It was like he had been talking about me when he told about the feelings he'd had when his parents had gotten a divorce.

The thoughts and words danced around in my mind. For the first time I realized that I was secretly glad about the divorce. Just like Mote said: Now I had Mom all to myself. I guess that's why I felt some sort of responsibility for it all, like my wish had come true. I had wished it on them, so it was my fault. I lay there and thought about it in the dark.

Then I whispered to myself, "That's dumb," and smiled and felt good. Better than I had felt in a long time. I didn't live happily ever after or anything, I just felt better.

Dad was saying, "Did you ever meet Mote, Rachel?"

"Yes. He seemed very nice. He couldn't believe I was Chris's mother. He said I looked too young, didn't he, Chris? He said I didn't look old enough to have a grown son. He ate dinner with us once out on the patio and was very polite and mannerly."

"He buttered his corn with a knife," I said.

I got the look again and touched my forehead, just to be sure. Dad said, "But he killed Holder. He must be a violent man."

"He didn't kill Holder, Dad."

"From what I read, the police seem quite certain."

"Well, they're wrong," I said.

Dad patted the corners of his mouth with his napkin. "It is nice to be loyal to your friends, Chris. But you can carry loyalty too far. Sometimes, just when you think you have somebody all figured out, they will turn around and do something completely different. You can never be sure about people."

I said, "Some people you can."

When Detective Stienert came I introduced him to my parents. He said, "How do you do" to my mother. He and my father clasped hands, hooking their thumbs at shoulder level and pumping their arms from side to side. Stienert grinned and said, "All *right*." I went into my room and got the pictures and put on a jacket. I kissed Mom and shook hands with Dad in the conventional manner.

We got into Stienert's car. There was a red light on the seat between us and a police radio on the dash, crackling with static noises. Stienert pulled away from the curb.

I said, "How come you don't squeal your tires like a real policeman?"

Stienert said, "You already eat?"

"I could eat some more." I could always eat some more. There was never a time when I couldn't eat some more.

"You like seafood?"

"Yes."

"Your mother very pretty."

"Thank you."

Stienert didn't drive on the main roads. He used side streets, turning every few blocks.

"Father seem like a nice guy."

I said, "I never saw him shake hands like that before."

"Means he hip. Know what happening."

I said, "You're leaving out words again. Didn't they have an English department at Eastern?"

"I was a bad influence on all the white boys at Eastern." He pulled into the Oasis restaurant. "We go on road trips. A few days and all the white guys talking like us, even the coach."

We got out of the car. Stienert carried a black radio with him. "I axed the coach what kind of player I would be guarding and Coach say, 'He be tall.' "

Stienert held up two fingers and the hostess showed us to a booth toward the back. The waiter put down water, silverware, and menus. Stienert said, "Don't worry about price. This on the department."

"How come?"

"Told them I need some money for an informant. They give me a hundred dollars."

I said, "What do you do with the change?"

"Give it back."

"Really?"

"Of course I give it back. What you think?"

"Sorry I axed."

We ordered shrimp cocktails and the red snapper dinners. In the next booth, over Stienert's shoulder, a little boy was banging a spoon on his high-chair tray. His mother's back was toward me.

Stienert said, "How come you don't like Baker?"

"I don't dislike him. You seem smarter."

The shrimp came. Stienert said, "Baker a good cop. A little rough. Worries about his bowels."

The little boy was trying to climb out of his high chair. His mother had to grab him. A man and woman were seated at a nearby table and the woman turned around to look at the little boy.

I handed Stienert the metal box and he looked at the pictures while we ate the shrimp. "Where you get these?"

"I'd rather not say."

Stienert looked up. "Tell me where you get them."

I said, "I don't want to. You wouldn't like it and it doesn't make any difference."

"Make a big difference," he said. "That Holder's wife?"

"Uh-huh."

"Who the man?"

"I don't know. You never get a good look at him, but you

can almost see the license number. I thought maybe you could make enlargements. Blow them up and make out the number."

Stienert looked at the pictures again, "Maybe," he said. "Where you get these?"

I took a deep breath. "The way I got them was probably breaking the law. I'd rather not tell you about it."

Stienert said, "Hmm."

The kid behind him cried out and the lady turned around to stare at him again. She turned to her husband and said something about poorly behaved children. The kid's mother heard it too and picked her son out of the high chair and held him next to her.

Stienert was angry. The snapper came and we ate in silence. "This is really good," I said.

Stienert nodded.

I said, "How many cases are you working on?"

"Four or five."

"Murders?"

"Uh-huh. The others all drug killings. Cocaine." He took a drink of water. "You ever mess with coke?"

"No. I don't even know what to do with it."

Stienert said, "What you do with cocaine, you run out of it."

"Is that when the trouble starts?"

He said, "Who else know about the pictures?"

I said, "Come on. Let up on me, will you? Just be glad you've got the pictures and see where they lead you. What difference does it make how I got them?"

"Make a big difference," he said. "Make a big difference who know about them, who had them, who made them."

I said, "Will anything I say be used against me?"

"Where you get that?" Stienert said. "You be watching *L.A. Law*? Forget that stuff. We just two guys eating fish."

"All right." I told Stienert about sneaking into Holder's house and where Billy had found the pictures. I told him about the hate literature in Holder's desk and about some guys coming in to clean out the desk while I was upstairs.

Stienert said, " 'Jesse Jackass'?"

"Uh-huh."

Stienert laughed. "He is kind of a jackass, a professional Negro."

"I thought all you . . . I thought all black people liked Jesse Jackson."

"Do all white people like Teddy Kennedy, Jerry Falwell?"

The little boy was facing us. I smiled and waved at him and he ducked his head. When he looked back up he spotted Stienert's hair and reached out to touch it. Stienert felt it and smiled.

"He like my Afro," he said, and leaned his head closer to the child.

The kid felt it some more. He looked at his mother and said, "Kitty, kitty."

His mother apologized to Stienert. "I'm very sorry."

Stienert said, "It's okay."

The mother made the little boy sit down and he squirmed and cried, trying to get back at Stienert's head. The lady at the table turned around again. She looked at the little boy like he smelled bad, and with her tongue, made a noise like *"Tsk, tsk."*

Stienert looked at the lady and said, "Why don't you turn around?"

"I beg your pardon?"

"Turn around and eat your food. Not polite to stare at people."

The lady said, "That child's behavior is rude. He's disturbing our meal."

Stienert said, "You disturbing my meal, the way you acting. Kid don't know no better, just being a kid. But you a grown-up."

She looked at her husband and he didn't say anything. Then she looked at Stienert and said, *"Humph."* She turned back to her husband. "I think we should go."

They stood up.

Stienert said, "Have a nice day."

The lady said *"Humph"* again. Her husband looked at his shoes.

Stienert looked through the pictures again. "I'm going to have to tell Baker about this," he said. "He'll be cool about it. He likes you boys. We checked up on both of you. Checked up on Holder a lot too."

"Find anything?"

"Holder an asshole. He in ERWA."

"In what?"

"ERWA. E-R-W-A. Means Equal Rights for White Americans."

I said, "Never heard of them."

"They new. Kind of Ku Klux Klan without sheets. Call themselves a political-action committee. Want to run their own candidates for office next year. Ol' Holder, he wouldn't like it, you being friends with Leon and his family."

"How do you know about that?"

"We ask around the neighborhood, find out about you and Leon and Billy. Find out that some of your best friends are colored, like a good liberal. You call yourself a liberal?"

"No," I said. "I call myself Chris."

Stienert paid the check and left a five-dollar tip. He put the change in an envelope and sealed it. When we got back in the car he said. "You gonna turn pro, after college?"

"No, I don't think so."

"Lots of money in the pros," he said. "You really good."

"I look good in the city championships," I said. "I'll do pretty good in college too, but the pros are something else. It's a whole different level of play."

"Know what you mean. I went one-on-one with Michael Jordan in a pick-up game. I had to guard him. When he wanted to score, he just scored. I'd have needed a flame thrower to stop him."

We drove up to my house. The lights were off and Dad's car was gone. Stienert said, "Your folks getting back together?"

"I don't know. I don't think they know."

"Would you like them to?"

"Yeah. Yeah, I would, if it was what they really wanted."

" 'Fraid to get your hopes up?"

"Something like that. I used to want them to get back together real bad. Now I don't mind it very much. Mote kind of helped me get through some of that stuff."

"How'd he do that?"

"Just talking," I said. "And something Mote said once. He said you never really start to grow up until you can look at your parents objectively, see them as they really are."

Stienert said, "Pretty heavy stuff."

"Yeah."

"My old man a drunk," Stienert said. "A mean drunk too. But when I think of him, you know, I only think of the good times. Like when he was sober and nice."

"Me too. I mean, Dad never got drunk or mean or anything. But like tonight, every once in a while I would catch him giving me this look of his. I call it the 'Immobilizer.' When he gives me that look I feel like he hates me."

"My daddy, he looked at me sometimes like, Who the hell are you? Sometimes I think he forgot he had kids."

I opened the door. "Thanks for the meal. Will you call me, keep in touch?"

"Yeah, I'll call you. Don't you go breaking into any more houses, Little Moon. No more teenage detective."

"Okay, Moon."

Mom had laid a note on my bed. It said:

> Chris,
> Mr. Sweeny called. He's in town and wants to talk to you.
> I told him to be at the house tomorrow at five.
> Love,
> Mom

▲ 8 ▲

BILLY AND I had final exams Monday. I told Billy about my evening with Stienert. "You forgot to tell him something," Billy said. He pointed to the front of the room where Mr. Douglas was standing. "You forgot to tell him about Mr. Douglas and Mrs. Holder."

Other students were filing into class, reading textbooks, cramming in last-minute information. Billy said, "You ready for the exam?"

"I'm always ready for exams."

Mr. Douglas began calling the roll. I slumped down in my seat, relaxing my shoulders. I closed my eyes, slowed my breathing, and made my mind go blank.

The first part of the exam was multiple-choice. I knew some of the answers right off and most of the others were easy to figure out by reading the question carefully and omitting obvious wrong choices.

Part two required single-word answers to questions. Some of the questions were difficult, but the answers dropped into place for me. I was a good test-taker. Billy and I used to study together the night before exams and Billy would know the material much better than I. Yet I would score in the nineties, while Billy scored in the eighties. I somehow came up with the answers and wished that I could teach Billy how to do it.

Taking tests was like playing tennis. I had to try hard

without trying too hard, letting the answers come instead of forcing them.

Part three required an essay answer about John Steinbeck, and I ate that one up. I had read everything Steinbeck wrote, before he was assigned to us as required reading. My essay was so good I worried that it would be over Mr. Douglas's head.

I finished the exam and looked up. Billy was staring out the window, drifting and daydreaming. No one had turned in an exam yet and I thought that I might as well be first. I walked between rows of bowed heads. Several students looked up at me with pleading eyes. Mr. Douglas watched me approach his desk. I handed him my papers and said, "Nice exam, Mr. Douglas."

Mr. Douglas said, "Thank you."

I said, "How is Mrs. Holder doing?"

Mr. Douglas said, "I don't know. How would I know?" He looked at me hard. There was a slight flush along the sides of his neck.

"I just wondered," I said. I walked out of the room, got a drink at the fountain, and said, "Ah-hah!"

Chuck came out of the classroom and got a drink. He had his camo outfit on. His trousers had about twenty pockets in them and his safari jacket had loops to hold bullets for his elephant gun. He said, "That last question—he's the guy who wrote *The Old Man and the Sea*, isn't he?"

I lied to him. "Yeah, that's him." No use ruining his day.

Chuck smiled. "Whew." He walked away, happy as can be.

Ten minutes later Billy came out looking pale and tired. He asked, "How did you do?"

"Fine." I told him about Mr. Douglas.

"How come you left so early?"

"I was through."

"You should check your answers," Billy said. "You should go back over the exam when you're done."

"I never do that."

We walked to our next exam room. I asked Billy what he

was doing tomorrow and he told me that he and his mother were going to visit his grandparents on the farm. "I can't get out of it," he said. "It's been planned for a long time. What are you going to do?"

"Thought I'd nose around a little. I want to find out more about ERWA. See if Stienert's found out who owned the VW."

"Wish I could stay," Billy said.

I said, "Maybe I'll watch Mrs. Holder. Follow her around. See if she meets with Mr. Douglas or the mystery man again."

The final exam of the day was American History, my favorite subject and my favorite teacher, Miss Lassiter. I finished first again and took my papers up to the front desk. She had a pretty smile. "Finished already, Chris?"

"Yes, ma'am, almost. I didn't fill out number sixteen."

Miss Lassiter read from the test sheet. "Who wrote the Declaration of Independence?" She looked up. "Why, you know that, Chris. It's the easiest question on the exam."

"Yes, ma'am." I said. "I know that the answer you want is Thomas Jefferson, but I don't think he wrote it."

"You don't? Who do you think *did* write it?"

"Thomas Paine. I think Thomas Paine wrote it for Jefferson and Jefferson copied it."

"My, my. Aren't you the scholar?" She gave me a knowing smile—she knew exactly what I was up to. What she didn't know was that I had dreams about her, the kind of dreams that are called erotic. The dreams were so vivid and intense that I had trouble looking her in the eye for several days. I had given her a pretty thorough working over.

"It's not my idea," I said. "I didn't think of it. Some real historians think it's possible and I read their arguments. They're pretty convincing."

"I didn't know that."

Miss Lassiter took a red marker and put a big X next to number sixteen. She looked up at me and smiled. "That's for being such a kiss-ass," she whispered.

I said, "Yes, ma'am."

I walked out to the hall, blushing and nervous and suddenly realized that I was a senior. Bang, just like that. In the men's room I studied myself in the mirror. Still looked the same. I sure felt different but didn't know if it was being done with school for the summer or the Miss Lassiter thing. Maybe she had dreams about me! Probably not.

I walked down the front steps and turned around to look at the school, feeling sad and happy. That sting-y feeling was in my eyes and as I walked home I felt like a very little boy.

The refrigerator was absolutely full and there was nothing to eat in it. When in doubt, eat pasta. I put on some water to boil and chopped up some onions and peppers. While the noodles cooked I sautéed the onions and peppers in butter. I poured the spaghetti into a colander to drain, then dumped it into the frying pan and put a lid on it. The smell of the peppers and onions had my stomach going, but I made myself wait while they simmered together a little longer. Tremendous self-discipline.

I ate the spaghetti and dialed police headquarters. When I got through to Stienert I said, "Got another suspect for you."

"Who you got, Little Moon?"

"Aren't you going to bribe me? Get another hundred dollars?" I took another forkful of spaghetti. It was very good.

"Tell me what you got first."

I told him about seeing Mr. Douglas leave with Mrs. Holder on the day of the funeral.

"Maybe he just consoling the bereaved widow."

"Could be. But today, after the exam, I asked him how Mrs. Holder was doing and he got kind of excited. He turned red and said, 'How would I know?' "

"That's all? Man turns red? That's your suspect?"

"More than you had before. I call that first-class detective work."

"Haw."

"How about you? You find out who owns the VW?" If I had some cheese, the spaghetti would have been better. Mushrooms.

"Got a list. Couldn't make out all the numbers. Just got a list of possibilities."

"Who's on it?"

"Can't tell you, Little Moon. Can't give that out."

"Why not?"

"It be police business. Despite the first-class detective work, you still not a policeman. What you gonna take in college?"

"Black English," I said. "I want to learn to say things like 'It be police business.' "

Stienert laughed. "I think you should major in Wise Guy. That what you best at."

"I don't think you're being fair. I'm giving you all these surefire leads, all these clues, and all you do is give me this it-be-police-business jive."

"Sorry, Little Moon. Baker'd have my butt up a rope if I tell you."

"He wouldn't know," I said. "Come on, Brother Moon. How about ERWA—you find anything about them?"

"Yeah. They not secret or anything. Meet right at the YMCA every month."

"Are you going to infiltrate their organization?"

"Not none of me, man. I think they be suspicious, a black dude come to their meetings. Might put two and two together, figure I not sincere in my convictions."

"When do they meet?"

"Wait a minute."

I heard Stienert rustle some papers. I finished off the spaghetti and stretched the phone over to the refrigerator and stared into it. No luck. Stienert said, "They meet tomorrow night. They meet every month on the last Tuesday."

"I'll go to the meeting," I said.

"Don't do that, Little Moon. Don't do that. They not violent or anything, but you never know. I mean, they not the PTA either. Let us do the police work. We'll wrap this case up in a couple days."

"What do you mean, wrap this up? Are you about ready to arrest somebody?"

Stienert was silent for a moment. "Listen, Little Moon" —his voice was lowered—"I know Mote a friend of yours and all that, but he still the prime suspect. He's been seen. Baker going to search for him tomorrow."

"Where is he?"

"I'm sorry, Little Moon. Can't tell you that."

"It be police business, right?"

"Yep."

"Nuts."

"Sorry."

After I hung up I said, "Nuts" to the empty house. It didn't help. Neither did washing my face and staring into my own eyes. I wondered if they would catch Mote. Would he try to get away? Would they shoot at him?

I lay on my bed and thought. Then I stood up, put my hands in my hip pockets, and paced back and forth. I looked out the window and rocked on my heels and chewed the inside of my lips. I needed to borrow a car. I dialed.

Sampson answered the phone. I asked him if Leon and I could go fishing tomorrow and he told me that Leon had to work. I probably could have used his car but didn't want to ask.

I tried Mr. Sherman's number and got no answer.

Mom's boyfriend at the used-car lot gave me some talk about insurance regulations. It was probably true. I said, "Thanks anyway," hung up, and went back to talking to myself. What kind of detective doesn't even have a car?

I dialed again.

A little girl's voice said, "Hello."

I said, "May I speak to Vicki, please?"

"Whom may I say is calling?"

"Chris Miller. Tell her Chris is calling."

She giggled and laid down the phone. I could hear her yell, "Vicki, it's him," and it made me feel better. There was some hushed conversation in the background.

"Hello."

I imitated the little girl. "Vicki, it's him."

She said, "I'll kill her. This time I'll kill her."

"Don't do that. It was very nice, really. Flattering."

"Do you have a sister?"

"No."

"Give thanks," she said. There was a slight click on the line. Vicki said, "Hang up, Stacy." Silence. "Hang up or I'm coming after you." There was another click. "She's cute, Chris. That's the trouble—she's so darn cute that she gets away with it. No one can stay mad at her."

I should have said that she had to be cute, like her big sister, but I'm no good at sweet-talking girls. Instead I said, "How are you?"

"Fine. How about you?"

"Fine. I finished with school today. All of a sudden I'm a senior."

"Me too. Kind of scary, huh?"

"Yeah," I said. "It is."

We talked about college plans. Vicki was going to Ohio State and I told her that I had a scholarship offer there but hadn't made up my mind. We talked about summer jobs and music and movies that we liked. She was nice to talk to, even though she liked chain-saw movies and Bruce Springsteen.

I took a deep breath. "Listen, Vicki, I'm going to ask you for a date. It's a really dumb date and you'll probably say no and I don't blame you."

"Ask anyway."

"Do you like to fish?"

"Uh-huh. I've been fishing with my dad. I like it."

"Well, would you like to go fishing with me tomorrow, early in the morning?"

"Gee, I don't know."

"I know it's short notice and it's a dumb first date, but I think you'd have a good time. I guarantee a good time."

"Guaranteed, huh?"

"Yes. There's one more thing. I don't have a car. I tried to borrow one but no deal. We would have to take your car."

"I have to ask my parents."

"Sure."

"Ten minutes," she said. "Call me back."

It was a long ten minutes. Stacy answered the phone again. She said, "I'm going fishing with you."

There were sounds of sisters wrestling for the phone. Vicki said, "Chris?"

"Hi."

"Good news and bad news," she said. "I can go, but we've got to take Stacy."

"That's fine, Vicki."

"You sure? You sure it's okay?"

"Very sure."

"And I have to drive."

"Great. Stacy and I will sit in back and make out."

She had a good laugh. Girls who laugh at my wisecracks all have good laughs. She said, "Okay, I'll fix us a lunch."

"Nope. No lunch."

"Why? You don't know Stacy. She's hungry all the time."

"I want to play the great provider. We'll eat some fish."

"What if they don't bite?" Vicki said.

"They'll bite. Bring something to drink, some lemonade or iced tea or something. I'll provide the rest."

I gave her my address. "Can you be here about seven?"

"Okay."

I said, "Good-bye," and Stacy yelled into the extension, "See you in the morning."

I hung up the phone and it rang immediately. I said, "Hello."

A husky voice said, "Is this Chris Miller?"

"Yes."

"Let's arrange to meet somewhere, Miller. You give me the ledger book."

"What ledger book?"

"The one you lifted from Ben Holder's desk yesterday."

"Who is this?"

"I'm a guy that does mean things to people, beat them up,

shoot them, things like that. You give me the book and none of that happens to you."

"What are you talking about?"

"Don't do that," Husky Voice said. "Don't play dumb, don't deny anything. You got the ledger, I want it. I'm going to get it. Unnerstand?"

"Understand," I said. "With a D."

"Huh?"

I said, "I really don't know anything about a ledger."

Husky Voice sighed. "All right, Miller. You've been warned. This is your first warning. You only get two."

I said, "What do you mean?" but the phone was dead.

I called Stienert back and told him about the phone call from Husky Voice. He said, "What is this ledger?"

"I don't know. The only thing I can figure is that it was in Holder's desk. Remember? I told you about some guys coming in and cleaning out his desk while I was hiding upstairs."

Stienert said, "Hmm."

"Getting complicated, huh?"

Stienert said "Hmm" again.

"What are you going to do?"

"I check around," he said, and hung up.

The best thing to do, I decided, was to take a nap.

▲ 9 ▲

I DREAMED that I was back in Holder's house, searching through his desk drawers. When I opened the bottom drawer I found the combination lock from our clubhouse and I popped awake wondering about it.

The lock! How did the killer get into the clubhouse to get Mote's knife?

I was still thinking about the dream and the lock when the doorbell rang. Through the curtains I saw a tall, high-shouldered fellow dressed in warm-up clothes. I said, "Who is it?" through the door.

"Bill Sweeny."

"Who?"

"Bill Sweeny, from Cassidy University."

"Oh, yeah." I opened the door. "Come in, Mr. Sweeny."

He walked in, looking very Irish, jet-black hair and square features. "Did your mother tell you I was coming over?"

"Yes, sir. Mom left me a note, and I'm sorry, I forgot about it. I've kind of had a lot going on today."

"Final exams?"

"Yes, sir. Finals."

We sat in the living room and talked for several minutes about tennis, the university, and academics. He said, "I watched you play Miles Crayton Saturday."

"You did?"

"You looked like you were getting tired in the last set."

"I was. I've been . . . a friend of mine has gotten into trouble. I've been missing sleep."

"Are you in good shape?"

"Yes, sir. I've never lost a match because of getting tired. Usually, I mean. If it goes five sets, I feel like I am going to win, for sure."

"That's what Mr. Sherman said. I talked to him after the match."

"Oh." The guy with the husky voice sounded very serious on the phone. I wondered what he meant about two warnings.

"—during your match," Mr. Sweeny was saying.

"What?" I said. "I'm sorry, what did you say?"

"I said it looked to me like you were showing off some during your match."

"Yeah, I was. I do that. It's something that I do."

Mr. Sweeny smiled. "I guess we all do."

There must be two groups that wanted Mr. Holder's ledger. One group has it and the other group thinks I've got it.

"Mr. Miller?"

"Huh?"

"How about it? Would you go play some doubles with me?"

"Now?"

"Yes, now."

"Sure."

I got my bag and we drove to the country club. I had only played there a few times, as a guest. We went into the men's locker room and began to change.

"I'm playing for money, Mr. Miller. Does that bother you?"

"How much?"

"A thousand dollars."

"Yeah, that bothers me some. Can you call the bet off, Mr. Sweeny?"

"Sure. Call me Bill, please."

"Call me Chris. Who do we play, Bill?"

"The club champs. Sullivan and Dennis. Do you know them?"

"No," I said. "Why did you set this up, Bill? Is this some kind of test I have to pass?"

"No test. I've seen you play, I like your game and you're the quickest kid I've ever seen. Your grades are good. I want you on my team. This is just a way to get to know each other."

The combination was eleven, twenty-nine, fifteen. It was typed on a piece of paper stuck on the back of the lock and I remembered peeling it off and throwing it away.

We met Dennis and Sullivan in the lounge. Dennis was a short, stocky fellow with a patch of baldness right on top. Sullivan was tall and willowy. Mr. Sweeny introduced me and we went out to court number one and began to warm up.

Sweeny was a left-hander and took the backhand court. His strokes were awkward and forced, but he hit the ball well. The three of them must have been old friends and kept up a steady stream of insulting conversation.

Dennis was a wristy player and slapped at his shots. He hit low shots well but avoided high-bouncing balls to his backhand. Sullivan had a weak backhand too but really smacked his forehands. They both volleyed well and had solid overheads, the kind of players who are best at doubles, especially if they play together as a team.

We met at net to spin for serve. I asked Dennis, "You're the club doubles champs, huh?"

"Uh-huh. Five years in a row."

I looked at Sweeny. He winked at me. We won the spin and Sweeny tossed me the balls. "Serve 'em up, Chris."

I served to Sullivan's backhand and came to net, thinking more about the dream than about tennis. Nobody was supposed to know the combination.

We lost the first game, mostly because Dennis and Sullivan guessed right every time and played good defensive tennis. I wasn't playing very well either. We changed sides after the first game.

Sweeny said, "Don't try to outthink these guys. Let the game come to you. Don't force anything and be patient."

I said, "I'm not used to losing my serve." I took a drink of water. "How should we play them?"

"Just play your game, Chris."

Sullivan had a funny service motion, the motion that is called "herky-jerky" in a baseball pitcher. He hit the first serve very hard into my body and I blocked the ball back at his feet as he came to net. His return was short and Sweeny cut in front of me and volleyed between them for a winner.

Some of the club members had wandered into the grandstand to watch the match. Most of them carried mixed drinks. Sullivan aced Sweeny, then he aced me. At forty–love Sweeny hit a blistering return of serve with his awkward-looking forehand that Dennis hit out long. Sullivan served to my backhand at forty–fifteen and I lobbed over Dennis's head. Sullivan crossed behind him and hit a nice backhand volley that Sweeny couldn't reach. It was two games to none.

Only Billy, Leon, Mote, and I knew the combination.

Sweeny had a wicked slice serve—the spin made it kick to my right. I was at net and began crossing before Sullivan made his swing. He saw me and tried too late to change his stroke. The ball hit into the net.

We won Sweeny's service game and sat down between games. Whoever it was must have worked the combination, picked up one of Mote's knives, closed the door, and locked it. The police had to break the lock to get in.

Dennis didn't serve hard, but he leaned into it and came to net fast behind it. He picked off my return and volleyed down at Sweeny's feet to win the point.

Sweeny played up for Dennis's serve and returned to Sullivan. Sullivan hit the volley at my left hip and I returned a weak blooper. Sullivan could have hit it anywhere he wanted for an easy point, but he smashed the ball at my stomach, hard. It didn't hurt much, but I let it make me mad. I play better when I'm mad.

I played up for Dennis's serve, like Sweeny did, chipping a low return at his feet as he came up to net. He hit a half volley that hung in the air and I smacked it at Sullivan. He turned his back and the ball hit him in the buttocks. It made a nice, solid popping noise. Sullivan didn't rub it. Tough.

I kept thinking about the husky-voiced guy. There was something about the way he spoke that bothered me a lot.

Sweeny said, "What are you thinking about, Chris?"

"Sorry." Sweeny had noticed. Probably a very good coach.

Dennis and Sullivan won the first set, but Sweeny and I won the second set easily. We were starting to play better as a team. Between the second and third sets we took a break. Sweeny and Dennis had beer, Sullivan had some kind of mixed drink. I sipped water. Dennis said, "You going to Cassidy, Chris?"

"I don't know yet, Mr. Dennis."

"If you decide on Cassidy, let me know. I own Tri-county Chevrolet. See that you get a nice car to drive."

"I can't afford a car."

Dennis said, "Don't worry, we can work something out."

I toweled off my arms. I had just witnessed a recruiting violation. Pretty slick, the way he did it.

The sun had gone down and we played the third set under the lights. Sweeny and I won the set and the match. Dennis and Sullivan had become tired toward the end, and Sullivan acted a little bit drunk. We sat in the lounge. There were some nice-looking ladies sitting around. Tanned tennis legs are hard to beat.

Sullivan had bourbon on ice, two of them. Sweeny and Dennis drank beer. I asked for iced tea.

Sullivan reached into a gym bag, pulled out a wallet, and peeled off five one-hundred-dollar-bills. Dennis began filling out a check. "How do I make this out?"

Sweeny said, "Make it to Cash."

The waiter brought over a platter of sandwiches.

Dennis made out the check and laid it on top of the five one hundreds. Sweeny picked up the check, folded it in half, and put it inside his racket cover. He pushed the bills toward me, about three inches closer.

"So what do you think, Chris?" He took a swallow of beer.

"About what?"

"About college, about Cassidy. I think you'd like it there."

I said, "I really haven't made up my mind, Bill." I looked at the money. "I'm not playing games or being cute. I just haven't decided. I have another year to decide."

Sweeny nodded. Dennis said, "I got a little Chevy I bet you'd like. Little Cavalier convertible, about twenty thousand miles on her."

"Easy payments on her?" I asked.

"Low payments," he said. "We could probably work something out. Maybe you could give me some tennis lessons. Do some work around the lot."

I took a drink of tea and spilled some on my shirt. Sweeny pulled out some papers. "This is a letter of intent," he said. He put the folded papers on top of the bills and slid it all over to me. "Why don't you look it over?"

I picked up the papers, leaving the bills on the table. I pretended to read the letter.

One time Mote had said, "Never do anything you would be ashamed of later on." Mote didn't moralize or preach. He just said that life wasn't as much fun if you had to live with that kind of thing in the back of your mind.

I turned the page. Dennis, Sullivan, and Sweeny were watching me. They seemed like nice guys. Dad had said, "Take the best offer, make the best deal you can."

I imagined myself in the convertible, driving her around— with five hundred dollars in my pocket. Sunglasses.

"I think I'll pass," I said. I slid the money toward Sweeny and took a drink of tea. Sweeny picked it up and put it in his pocket. Sullivan and Dennis looked at me like I was dumb. I felt kind of trembly and Sullivan said, "You sure?"

And I said, "Yes."

Sweeny and I showered without talking. He drove me back home. "I enjoyed the tennis," he said.

"Me too."

"Keep the letter of intent, Chris." He handed me an envelope. "You might change your mind."

"Sure." I watched him drive off. I walked up onto the front porch and the porch light exploded. A few pieces of glass showered down on my head and neck. A car engine started up across the street. The car drove off slowly with its lights off. The driver had pulled the sun visor down to the side, so I couldn't see his face.

I had trouble with the key but finally got it in the lock and turned it. Mom came into the living room. She said, "What was that noise?"

"The light. The porch light. I hit it accidentally with my racket."

"Oh. Where have you been?"

"I don't know."

"What do you mean, you don't know?"

"I mean, I've been playing tennis. I've been playing tennis with Mr. Sweeny, down at the country club."

Mom put her hand to her chest. "Scared me," she said. "That noise, I thought it was a shot."

The phone rang and Mom turned to get it. I peeked outside through the curtains. "It's for you, Chris."

I said, "Hello."

"Pretty good shot, huh?" It was the husky voice.

I didn't know what to say.

"That's your second warning, sport. How about it? How about giving me the ledger?"

"Jesus, mister. Listen, I really don't have the book. I believe you. I'm scared and I'd give you the book if I had it. I really don't have it."

Husky Voice was silent. I could hear him breathe in and out like he had some asthma. Finally he said, "Your buddy got it?"

"No."

"The way I hear it, the way my people tell it, you and some other kid went into Holder's house and got the ledger. They pay me to get it back."

"Listen," I said. I was talking in a husky voice myself. "Listen, okay, we did go to Holder's. While we were in there somebody else came. Two guys. I was upstairs. After they left I looked in the desk. It had been cleaned out. That's the truth, mister. Whoever came in got your ledger."

He breathed in and out some more, a little louder this time. For some reason, the breathing scared me more than the shot.

"It's a mistake to lie to me, partner."

"I'm not lying. That's the truth."

More breathing. I could hear traffic sounds in the background. He must have stopped at a pay booth. "I'll check on it," he said. "I'll check your story, morning glory. But hear this—you lying to me, I don't give you any more warnings. If I find out you're lying, I put the next one through your knee, maybe shoot your momma in the elbow."

"Mister, I swear—"

He hung up. I started for my room. Mom hollered from her bedroom. "Who was that, Chris?"

"It was . . . it was one of the policemen, Mom."

I laid the envelope down on the dresser. The flap was unsealed and I realized there was something else inside besides the letter of intent. I opened it wider. The five one-hundred-dollar bills were in there, brand-new bills.

I thought about calling Stienert. He would probably have to make a report of the shooting, maybe come to the house and look for the bullet and Mom would be scared. I decided to wait until tomorrow. No use both of us being scared.

Hundred-dollar bills are funny-looking.

▲ *10* ▲

VICKI WAS five minutes early and Stacy was cute, all right. *Adorable* would be more like it, but I never used that word. It sounded too kissy. We loaded all the gear and supplies in the trunk and Vicki drove. I turned around and asked, "How old are you, Stacy?"

"Ten," she said. "I'm going to be eleven though."

"Eleven, huh?"

Stacy stood on the floor in back, leaned between the seats, and said, "Why does everybody always ask me that?"

"Ask you what?"

"Ask me how old I am."

"Well," I said. "I guess it's pretty corny, but it's a way to start a conversa—to start talking."

"I know what *conversation* means."

Vicki said, "Stacy." She turned right onto Route 8.

Stacy said, "Why did you say it, if it's corny?"

"I read a book called *How to Talk to Your Girlfriend's Sister*. It said the first thing you are supposed to say is 'How old are you?' "

"Oh."

I said, "I want to tell you a story. You and Vicki."

Stacy stood between the seats again and looked up at me with blue eyes. She said, "Once upon a time—"

"Okay. Once upon a time—"

Stacy interrupted, "I read a book about how sisters' boyfriends are supposed to tell stories. They are supposed to start with Once upon a time."

Vicki looked at me and rolled her eyes. I decided to change *adorable* to *smart*. Maybe *too smart*.

"Okay. Once upon a time there were two boys named Chris and Billy," I began. "They wanted to build a little clubhouse down by the railroad tracks, and they met a man there called Mote." I told them the whole story while we traveled north, first through the suburbs, then into the country.

Vicki said, "So that's why we're going fishing."

"Yes, ma'am. If you want to turn back, if you want to go back home, it's okay. I wouldn't blame you."

Stacy said, "Is Mote nice?"

"Yeah, he's real nice."

We drove in silence. Vicki looked a little bit mad. She pulled into a FINA station, turned off the ignition, and twisted in her seat to look at me. "I don't know what I should do." We looked at each other. Her overbite was terrific.

Stacy said, "I gotta tee-tee." Cute again.

The girls went into the ladies' room while I pumped gas, paid the bill, and wiped the windows. We got back into the car. Vicki said, "Stacy says we can trust you. She says she likes you." She started the car and pulled back onto the highway heading north again. "I can't understand why."

The last two miles were on a dirt road. Vicki was a good driver, much better than I, and I told her so. We hit a bump and passed under some low branches that brushed the top of the car. Some campers had used our spot since we'd been there last year. They had left firewood and there were no empty bottles or cans.

I said, "First thing we do is set up camp and build a fire."

"Why do you want to build a fire?" Vicki asked.

"Smoke. I want to send up some smoke."

"In case Mote's around, right?"

"Uh-huh."

We built up a big fire and set up some folding chairs. I

sent Stacy down to the river with a pot for water and we poured it on the fire, raising a big smoldering billow of smoke.

"What if he doesn't see it?" Vicki said.

I shrugged. "Best I can do. Let's go fishing."

The girls took off their slacks. They had bathing suits underneath. Stacy had a red two-piece suit, the top puckered up where her breasts would be. I rigged the girls up with spin-cast outfits. Vicki knew how to cast and Stacy learned quickly.

"We'll wade the river," I said. "It will be cold at first, but you'll get used to it." We entered the stream. They both *eek*ed and *brrr*ed and complained about the chill, but not too much.

I had my fly rod with a small yellow popper on the end of the line. Once Mote had said, "Any color popper is okay, long as it's yellow." I began false casting and looked over at Stacy. She was frowning, reeling in her spinner, her tongue stuck out the corner of her mouth. I cast the popper into a backwater eddy, jerked the line, and made it gurgle and dance in the slow current. I hoped we wouldn't see any snakes.

Ten minutes later I cast next to a deadfall, worked the popper once, and a nice-sized smallmouth boiled up and took it. I flicked my wrist to set the hook, and he was on solid. *"Yee-haw!"* I yelled, and the smallmouth leapt two feet out of the water, disappeared, and jumped again. The girls screeched.

The smallmouth headed for the sunken tree and I kept the pressure on, turning him toward the girls. He leapt closer to them and they screamed again, the way girls should. The fish streaked by us, heading downstream.

I walked downstream with him and paid out a few feet of line. The smallmouth jumped again. The sun was behind him and his gills shone blood-red. Marveling at his strength and stamina, I felt him throb and beat and pull. I held the rod high, showing off just a little with a pose from the cover of *Sports Afield.*

The line knifed through the water as the fish ran to the left, then to the right, and the first round was over. He had tired and the next jump was clumsy and sluggish. I pulled in some line and he fought against it with faded strength. He made a last staggering stand at about twenty feet away, tugging with punch-drunk lunges like a fighter who is beaten and weary in the final round, still on his feet, fighting on heart and instinct.

I gained more line and brought him to my legs in knee-deep water. "About two pounds," I yelled to the girls. I slipped my thumb in his jaw and lifted him from the water.

The girls walked over and we met in midstream to admire the fish. "He's pretty," Stacy said. The top of her swimsuit had slipped down. Her small nipples were surrounded by goosebumps.

"It's a she, Stacy. See the way her belly is swollen up? She's full of eggs." I removed the hook from the side of her mouth. "I'm going to turn her loose."

"Oh, good," Vicki said.

I lowered the fish into the water and held her facing upstream, my hands under her belly. She flared her gills once, then twice, a deeper pull this time, and slowly swam away.

"She'll go back to her nest," I said.

"Will she have babies?" Stacy asked.

"Yep. She'll have a couple thousand babies."

"Wow."

I tied small poppers on the girls' lines. Stacy looked down at her chest. "My boobs are showing," she said.

Vicki said, "Stacy!" It was about the tenth time she had said "Stacy," and it wasn't having any effect.

We started wading back upstream. Stacy slipped and fell into the water facedown. She got back up and kept walking as if nothing had happened. Water dripped from her face and hair, and Vicki and I pretended we didn't notice. I got a kick out of it and hoped she would fall again.

Vicki walked close to me, like she belonged there. We approached the fallen tree where the fish had taken the popper. I led the girls out of the water onto the bank. "Let's see if we can find the nest."

We walked along the edge of the water. "It will look like a little crater, like on the moon, with some small pebbles around it." Stacy led the way, peering into the water. Vicki saw it first. The nest was in six inches of water, two feet out from the bank. She pointed to the nest and turned to look at me. I nodded and held my forefinger to my lips in a *shhh* gesture.

Then Stacy saw it. "What's that, Chris?"

"That's it, Stacy. You found it." We looked at the nest. "They carry those pebbles in their mouth. If you want, we can stand here real quietly and see if she comes back."

We laid our rods on the rocky bank. Stacy stood closest to the water, Vicki stood behind her, and I stood behind Vicki. I put my hand on Vicki's shoulder and she reached across and put her hand on mine. I could still see the smoke from our fire rising through the trees a quarter mile downstream. Vicki's hair smelled clean and the river smelled the way it always did.

In about three minutes the fish was there. I didn't see her swim to the nest—she just materialized in the place that I was looking. I wondered how they did that. I said, "She's back."

"Where?" Stacy said.

"Just keep looking at the nest, a little to the right."

"I see her," Stacy said. "I see her." She raised her hand to point and the fish swam off.

"She'll be back," I said. "You can't move though. They can see you when they're in shallow water."

A minute later Vicki said, "There she is."

I said, "That's not her. That's the male. They kind of take turns guarding the nest."

Stacy said, "Is that her husband?"

"Uh-huh."

The female returned, holding in the current with slow, graceful waves of her tail and pectoral fins. The male swam toward her, then away. The female drifted by the nest and hung suspended like she was looking at us. I gathered up my courage and kissed the back of Vicki's neck. She leaned back against me and made a soft humming sound. The male drifted in from deeper water and looked at us too, side by side with the female.

Stacy said, "Isn't that romantic?"

Vicki said, "Yes," and smiled at me.

If the kid hadn't been there . . .

There was a deep-water pool upstream from the deadfall. I put the girls in good casting positions and let them work the water with their poppers. Stacy got a hit. The fish jumped and threw the hook before she knew it was on. Stacy said, "Aw, nuts."

Some crows flew over, chasing an owl. In the middle of the pool several minnows jumped and rippled the top of the water. Vicki said, "Did you see that?"

I said, "Cast over there real quick. There's probably a bass under there chasing the minnows." Vicki cast and the bass hit her lure the moment it hit the water. Vicki said, "Ooh, ooh," and began cranking her reel. Her rod tip bent against the weight of the fish. "Help me, Chris."

"Nope, your fish. Lift your rod up. Let the bend of the rod fight the fish for a while. Don't crank so fast."

She slowed down her retrieve. The bass broke water, about twelve inches long, right about a pound. "This is the fun part," I said. "Enjoy it. Take your time."

I like to watch people catch fish. Vicki was totally involved with the fish now, forgetting Stacy and me, unaware that she was being looked at. Stacy watched the line saw back and forth through the water. "Don't let him get away," she said.

I waded over by Vicki. The fish was tiring and she was

reeling in slowly. She looked up at me and smiled. "Bring him over to me," I said. "Don't force him—just lead him."

The fish was beaten. It let Vicki guide it toward me without a struggle. Vicki said, "It's kind of sad, isn't it?"

"Yes." I slipped my thumb in the fish's mouth. "You do it with your thumb and watch out for the hooks." I lifted the fish from the water.

"Are you going to let him go?" Vicki said.

"Up to you. You caught him."

"Let him go."

Stacy said, "Can I do it?"

"Sure," I said. "Wet your hands. Never touch a fish with dry hands, it's bad for them. Wipes off their protective slime and they get a skin disease."

Stacy dipped her hands in the water and I handed her the fish. "Feels like snot," Stacy said.

Vicki said, "Oh, Stacy."

Stacy looked at me quickly and caught me grinning, so she said "Feels like snot" again.

I let go and the bass rested a moment, then slipped from Stacy's hands. She said, "Slicker than snot on a doorknob."

Vicki said, "Stacy, please."

We waded upstream. "What are we going to eat?" Vicki said. "We keep turning all the fish back loose."

"We'll catch some pan fish," I said. "Upstream. I know a place upstream."

Stacy said, "I'm having fun."

I said, "Me too," and wondered if she ever took a nap.

There was a pointed rock at the head of the pool that split the current and created an area of still water in its wake. On her third cast Stacy hit the rock with her lure and it dropped into the water, drifted uncertainly, then began floating downstream. Stacy twitched her rod, the popper popped, and the bass hit, just like it says in the how-to-fish books. Stacy was magnificent, playing the fish like an old pro. Vicki watched her sister with a look on her face that made me like her more than I already did.

I thumbed the fish, removed the hook, and let Stacy return her to the water. She said, "Nothing sad about it."

We pushed our way upstream to a sharp bend in the river that caused a turn-around in the current under a steep, under-cut bank. The turbulence created bubbles that floated and circled like a merry-go-round. Something about the place attracted redeyes, a small chunky fish that was great eating. I tied on a small woolly worm, cast into the edge of the bubbles, and let the current drift the fly. There was a tug and the fish was on.

I stripped in line, palmed the redeye, and put him on my stringer. I cast back into the bubbles. "If we're careful, if we don't spook the fish, we can catch our lunch right here."

Vicki sat down on a rock ledge and turned her face up to the sun and leaned back with her eyes closed. She had long, slender legs that came together in a V that I couldn't stop glancing at when Stacy wasn't looking. Very good legs. Stacy stood by my side. She said, "I think your fish was the biggest, Chris."

"Maybe." Another redeye hit and I stripped him in.

"I think my fish was the prettiest," she said.

"I think so too."

I caught nine redeyes before they quit biting and the stringer was heavy. We walked over to Vicki and tied the stringer to a sycamore root, letting the fish sway in the current. "You guys getting hungry?"

They were. We left our rods and walked up the bank. "There's a little feeder stream up here," I said. We ducked under an overhanging bush. "Last year it was loaded with watercress."

I lifted Stacy over a fallen maple tree and gave Vicki a hand. When she bent over I got a look down the top of her suit. The feeder stream was about three feet wide and tree limbs grew across it to form a tunnel. Stacy said, "It's cold."

"Yeah, it's from a spring." We stopped to drink from cupped hands. Vicki had light brown hair on the backs of her arms.

We waded around the bend and stood up. The spring creek was choked with watercress and Mote was sitting on the grass, smiling at us.

▲ *11* ▲

STACY SAID, "Is that the guy?"

I said, "Yeah, that's the guy." Mote and I hugged shoulders. We had never done that before.

The girls sat down on the grass and took off their sneakers. I handed them each a few sprigs of watercress and watched their faces as they discovered the spicy, hot flavor.

Mote looked tired. I said, "One of the detectives told me that you've been spotted. They're going to search for you."

Stacy climbed down to the spring and squatted to pick more watercress. I took a mesh sack out of my vest pocket and joined her. We filled the sack together. "You getting hungry, Stacy?"

"Uh-huh. This stuff won't hold me for long."

"Let's go eat, Mote."

We began wading back downstream. I went over all the details of the Holder case with Mote, and he listened closely while he scanned the banks, glancing back and forth and turning to look behind us. Vicki waded along beside me and our arms brushed together now and then.

I said, "Who did you give knives to, besides Billy and me?"

Mote said, "I've been thinking about that. I can't remember everybody. The man at the hardware store took six on consignment and I don't know if he sold any. I gave one to Leon and traded one at the tackle shop for dry-fly hooks."

Stacy had caught a redeye all by herself and we added it to

87

the stringer. We stopped at an underwater rock shelf and Mote showed the girls how to jig along the edges.

The fire had burned down to a bed of coals. I raked some coals aside and took the potatoes out of the trunk. They were wrapped in foil and I dropped them into the coals. Mote said, "Have you got some kind of bowl? I'll clean the fish."

I handed Mote a plastic bowl. Mote asked Stacy, "Would you like to watch?" and Stacy said, "I don't know."

Mote pulled his knife out of a sheath and ran a sharpening stone over it. Stacy said, "Did you stab that fella?"

Mote said, "No." He put the stone away and turned to walk back to the river. Stacy watched him, then went skipping down to join him. Mote held her hand and Stacy looked up at him.

I got out a frying pan, cornmeal, and peanut oil. Vicki put the watercress in a large Tupperware bowl. She kept turning to look toward Stacy and Mote while she worked.

I said, "Stacy will be all right."

She said, "I know."

"There's a jar of salad dressing in the trunk."

Vicki found the jar, shook it, and dipped a finger into it and tasted. "Good."

I said, "You don't talk much."

"This is all new to me, Chris. Meeting murder suspects in the woods, wading rivers, getting kissed on the back of my neck. I've been more the go-to-the-show-and-hold-hands type."

"It's kind of new to me too. I'm more the go-fishing-with-the-boys, sit-around-and-talk-dirty type."

Vicki added some sticks to the fire and brushed her hands. "Do you always sweep girls off their feet on the first date?"

I said, "No. That's new for me too. I'm sort of getting swept myself." I looked at Vicki and she looked back at me.

Mote and Stacy came up from the river with a bowl of fillets. I squeezed the potatoes. They had started to soften, and I added a few more coals and set the frying pan on the grill.

Stacy said, "You should have seen it, Vicki. Blood and guts and everything."

Vicki said, "Did you like it?"

"Uh-uh." Stacy shook her head. "But Mote said that's what happens if you eat meat. Something has to die and somebody has to cut it up."

Mote wandered off up the tractor road by the cornfield. The oil began to smoke and I put in some fillets. Stacy came over with the plates. "Listen to them sizzle, Stacy."

Stacy made a slurping sound with her mouth. I said, "Take a stick and rake those potatoes out of the coals." I turned the fish over. They were just right, golden-brown, flaking slightly at the edges. I added some more fillets to the skillet.

Camp-cooked meals can be very bad. Things get burned or undercooked or the fire won't act right. They can also be perfect, forever-memorable meals, and this one was as good as the best. It was impossible to eat without bragging about it.

Vicki said, "It must be the cook."

I said, "No, it's something about cooking outdoors."

We tossed our paper plates into the fire and watched them burn, the edges catching first with a blue flame, then yellow, then red. Mote and I took the grill and skillet down to the river while the girls straightened up around camp.

"What are you going to do, Mote?"

"Better not stick around here," he said.

"Why don't you head up north, into Canada or something?"

Mote scrubbed the skillet with sand and gravel. "Feel like I need to stick close for a while. See how all this comes out. It's time I quit running." He rinsed the skillet in the current, "Twenty years is a long time to run, and I'm tired of it."

"Running from what, Mote?"

"The 'Nam stuff."

"Pretty bad, huh?"

He bent over to scoop up water with his hands and splash his face. "Bad enough that I can't remember some of it."

I said, "Do you try?"

"All the time. Well, not all the time. Not all the twenty years. For a long time I just ran away from it, stayed to myself, became a loner. Nobody needed me and I didn't need anybody. Then a few years ago something happened that got me . . . that made me start trying."

"What was that?"

Mote wiped his face dry with a blue bandanna. "Can't you guess?"

I thought for a second. "No, what?"

Mote rinsed the bandanna and tied it around his neck. "You really don't know, do you?"

"No, of course not. I only see you a few weeks each year."

Mote picked up the skillet. "It's getting closer, especially the last few days. Sometimes I feel like I've almost got ahold of it. Then it slips away again."

The girls were gathering firewood. Mote kicked the fire together with the side of his shoe. Stacy dropped an arm-load of wood and asked me if that was enough. "Not quite, Stacy. Let's try to leave more than we found when we got here."

She skipped back toward the woods. Mote said, "Neat little kid, huh?"

I said, "Yeah, I guess."

Mote spoke very softly. "She was about her age, maybe a little smaller."

"What?"

He watched Stacy enter the woods, then raised his hands and looked at his palms. After a moment his hands began to tremble and he lowered them to his sides.

"Mote, what did you say?"

"Nothing." He looked at me and frowned like he didn't know who I was. It made me feel scared.

"What is it, Mote?"

He pinched the bridge of his nose. "Jesus Christ."

"Are you okay?"

I could hear Vicki and Stacy laughing as they returned with firewood. Mote glanced up and I saw something had caught his eye, past the girls toward the cornfield. I looked and saw a dust trail heading toward us.

Mote put a hand on my shoulder. "Looks like I've got to run some more anyway." He pulled me to him and hugged me hard, his face pressed against my neck. "I think it's about over." He pulled away and smiled at me.

I didn't know what to say. Mote tapped me lightly on the chin, turned, and ran into the woods.

We stacked the firewood and the girls sat down on the folding chairs. The car turned along the side of the cornfield and came toward us. The driver was taking the rutted tractor road too fast and the sedan bounced and bottomed out a couple of times. It stopped next to Vicki's car and three men got out. Two of the men had big wide hats like game wardens wear. The other man was Lieutenant Baker.

Baker strolled up to the fire, wiping his forehead with a handkerchief. His wig had slipped to the side a little bit and I wanted to reach up and straighten it for him. He put his hands on his hips and said, "What are you doing here?"

"Fishing," I said. "And eating. You just missed a great meal."

Baker gave me his hard stare. The two wide hats stood behind him. "Is Thomas around here?"

I said, "No."

Baker turned to the wide hats. "Take a look around."

The wide hats strolled away from camp. Baker stuck out his jaw. It was a new look he had worked up since the last time I'd seen him. He said, "You know what it means, aiding a fugitive?"

"Yes, sir."

He looked at Vicki and Stacy. "How about it? You girls see a man around here? About forty-five years old? Got a scar like the kid here, under his eye."

Vicki said, "No," and Stacy shook her head. Baker tried his new, mean jaw-out stare at them and Stacy stuck her jaw back out at him.

Baker nodded at Vicki. "That your girl?"

I looked at Vicki. "Yeah."

Baker tugged at my sleeve. "Come over here. I want to talk to you alone."

I asked the girls to load the car. Baker and I walked down to the river. There were two sets of footprints on the bank, Mote's and mine, from when we had carried down the grill and skillet. I walked in Mote's prints and Baker didn't notice.

Baker said, "Look, kid, Thomas is a wanted man. He's wanted for murder."

I picked up a flat stone and skipped it across the river. Three big skips, then a series of little skips.

Baker put his hands on his hips and looked around. Vicki was bent over, putting folding chairs in the trunk. He said, "Your girl's got a sweet little ass on her."

It made me mad, but I didn't say anything. Baker kept looking at her. She bent over again and Baker said, "Sweet."

I said, "I wish you wouldn't say those kinds of things about her."

"Huh?"

"About Vicki. I mean, I say that kind of thing about girls too, but . . . you know, some girls are special."

Baker took a deep breath and let it out. "If those girls weren't here, I'd cut me a switch and blister your bottom right here."

"What for?"

"Mashing around in Mote's footprints, for one thing." He put a big hand on my shoulder and shoved me up the bank. "Get those girls out of here. Go home."

We walked up toward the fire. Baker yelled, "Sid, Joe," and whistled through his teeth. I finished loading the car. When the guys with wide hats came back from the woods, Baker said, "Get on the radio, tell them to get Hester, and have him bring the bloodhounds. We got a fresh trail."

Vicki and I got back in the car. Stacy was lying down in the back. Wading a river make me tired too.

Vicki said, "Is everything all right?"

"No. Baker's bringing in dogs to track Mote."

Vicki started the car, "So what's next?"

"I'm going to an ERWA meeting tonight. See what that's like. See if anyone talks about Holder."

"Didn't you tell me that Detective Stienert told you not to go?"

"Uh-huh. That was before this happened. I can't let Mote go to jail. Stienert will understand."

"He's nice. He likes you. He talked about you and your friend while we watched the tennis match."

"Billy?"

"Yes. And Leon. He thinks it's nice the way you treat Leon." She turned onto Route 8 and headed south. "Maybe you shouldn't go to that meeting, Chris."

"I'll be careful."

"Stacy says you're the best boyfriend I've had." She checked her mirror and pulled around an old Pontiac. The rear springs were shot and the car swayed and sagged as it smoked down the road. It reminded me of the way Mrs. Crowly walked. "Did you mean that when the detective asked if I was your girl? You said yes. Did you mean that, or was it just something you said."

"Well, yeah. I think I mean it, I mean, if it's okay."

She kept her eyes on the road. "It's okay."

"The thing is, Vicki, you've seen me at my best. You've watched me play tennis and fly-fish. Those are my best things. It might be downhill from now on as you get to know me better."

"What else are you good at?"

"That's it. Wait until you hear me try to sing or see me try to draw. I'm terrible at football and my knees shake when I have to give a speech. I can't wiggle my ears or do card tricks either. At parties I sit in the corner and sulk. And I'm not nice. I'm arrogant and smart-alecky. I'm not nice with Leon either. I tease him a lot."

She reached over her hand and I held it and we drove a half hour without talking. I like girls who don't have to talk all the time.

▲ *12* ▲

I GOT MY basketball and caught the bus to the YMCA. It was still light enough to shoot baskets on the outdoor courts and I worked on jump shots. I was terrific on a basketball court by myself, but in a game, with someone guarding me and people yelling, I come apart. I hit a jumper from eighteen feet. There was no net on the basket and it wasn't as satisfactory.

A pickup truck with big tires pulled into the lot and parked. A short fellow in cowboy boots carried in some boxes. Two more cars pulled in and the men got out of their cars and stood by the back door, talking.

I made some lay-ups, about three feet short of dunking the ball. *How do they do that?*

Another pickup pulled in and two more guys joined the group. One of them was real tall, six feet four or five. He watched me over his shoulder and then sauntered over. I tossed him the ball and he took a shot that rolled the rim.

I got the rebound and missed a fifteen-footer. The big guy made a few dribbles, drove to the basket, and rolled in a lay-up. The short guy with boots came over and the tall guy passed him the ball. I said, "You guys going to work out?"

Shorty said, "No. We got a meeting."

The tall guy was trying to dribble behind his back and between his legs. You could tell he could have done it at one time.

"What kind of meeting?" I said.

"ERWA." Shorty said. "Equal—"

"—Rights for White Americans," I said.

Shorty was impressed. "Hey. You heard of us?"

"Uh-huh." I held the ball on my hip. "Guy I knew was in it. The guy who was murdered."

"Holder," the tall guy said. "Ben Holder."

"Yeah, that's him." I took a hook shot and missed. "He said I ought to come to one of the meetings, and I said I'd like to. Sounds interesting. I didn't know you met at the Y. I thought you were more secret."

"We're not secret," Shorty said.

"Is it okay if I sit in on your meeting?"

Shorty looked at Tall. Tall shrugged his shoulders. Shorty said, "Let me ask the other members," and flipped the ball to me. "What's your name?"

"Chris," I said. "Chris Miller and I sure do hate niggers."

Shorty smiled and walked off toward the meeting room.

I tried some shots from the free-throw line. Tall got down on one knee to tie his shoelace. "Do you really hate niggers, Chris?"

"Yeah, sure. I mean, I guess so. Don't you?" I passed him the ball.

"Of course not." He straightened up and tossed me the ball. "I just don't like some of the things that are going on. Things like this affirmative action, minority rights, all that."

I tossed the ball back to him. "How come you're in ERWA?"

"Somebody's got to look out for our rights too." He took a lefthanded hook shot and banked it perfectly. He tossed me the ball. "I've been with the same company for eight years. Last year I was due for a big promotion, big raise, but they gave it to a black guy instead. Guy had the IQ of a walnut, but they gave him the job anyway so they could have a black guy in a managerial position. Looks good on paper. You think that was fair?"

I missed a jump shot. "No."

Tall got the rebound. "It wasn't fair when it was the other

way around either. I know that, but still, I should have had that job." He took a long shot and hit it. "So I joined ERWA."

Tall and I took a few more shots in the fading light. He said, "Don't take these guys too seriously in the meeting."

I said, "Okay."

"Some of them get a little carried away, you know?"

"Uh-huh."

"Don't believe everything you hear. Just enjoy the meeting, then go out and chase girls, take in a movie."

Shorty came back with a white-haired man about sixty years old. He said, "Chris, this is Charley. Charley is in charge of new membership. He'll take care of you, show you around."

Charley shook my hand and we walked into the meeting room. There were some long tables in front with stacks of literature, small pamphlets, newspapers, and single-page mimeographed sheets.

"There's some good reading there," Charley said. "The truth—not all the propaganda you get in the regular papers." He picked up an assortment and handed them to me. There were a half a dozen men sitting in folding chairs, reading. Most of the members were standing outside, smoking and talking.

Charley said, "Let's have a seat. You want some coffee?"

We got coffee from a big steel urn and sat in the back row.

Charley said, "We need more young people like you. We need young men to help fight the white man's war."

"White man's war?"

"Yeah, it's a war."

"White versus black?"

"Yep. Of course, the blacks are just being used. The Jews are behind it all. The Jew Communists."

"I didn't think Jews were Communists."

"They keep it secret," Charley said. "They control everything— the White House, the Federal Reserve, the Trilateral Commission, all of Russia."

"How come Russia is so tough on the Jews, then?"

"That's just publicity."

"I see." I took a sip of coffee. "What is the Trilateral Commission?"

"An equalization board. They get together and decide who can buy land. Article Thirteen or Fourteen. I'm not sure."

Some more members strolled in. They said "Hi" to Charley, and looked me over. I didn't recognize anyone.

I said, "So how long have you been a member of ERWA?"

"About three years. Some niggers moved in next door three years ago and I joined up. Never thought it would happen in our neighborhood. They moved right next door, the niggers did."

"Is that all? They just moved in?"

"That's enough, ain't it? How would you like it if some nigger family moved in next to you?"

"Which nigger family?"

"Any nigger family."

I said, "Ray Charles."

"Huh?"

"Ray Charles," I repeated. "You said, 'Any nigger family.' Well, I'd take Ray Charles. I've always thought how nice it would be to live next to Ray."

"I don't mean that. I mean some niggers you don't know."

I thought about it. "Which side would they move in on?"

"I don't know. It don't matter, what side they move in on. Niggers are niggers."

"Well, it would matter to me. My best friend lives on one side, on the right. I'd hate to see him move away. His name is Billy. Now old lady Crowly lives on the left. Almost anybody would be an improvement on Mrs. Crowly."

Charley shifted around in his seat to face me. "I got daughters, two daughters."

"So?"

"You know."

"Know what?"

"You know what they say. You know, about black guys and white girls."

"Oh." The coffee was weak and I set my cup on the floor.

"Property values go down too," Charley said. "You know that. How would you like that, your property go down?"

"How much?"

"What?"

"How much would it go down?"

"Well, hell, I don't know for sure. I mean, I don't know the exact amount. What difference does it make?"

"It makes a lot of difference," I said. "Two, three dollars, I probably wouldn't get too upset. Five thousand wouldn't be too bad if you get Ray Charles. Somebody like Idi Amin would be a bad deal. Even if your property went up."

"Would you forget about Ray Charles?"

"You could leave your windows open," I said. "Listen to him practice. You like Ray Charles, don't you?"

"No."

"Really?" I turned to face him. "How about Bill Cosby? You watch *The Cosby Show*?"

"No, I don't. Those shows, those shows like *Cosby*—you know what they're trying to do?"

I thought a moment. "I guess they try to be entertaining."

Charley shook his head. "No, what they really try to do is make it look like nigger families are just like white families. They try to act like whites and blacks are pretty much the same."

I said, "Nobody would believe that."

"You'd be surprised," Charley said. "You'd be surprised at some of the dumb stuff people will believe."

A heavyset guy sat down next to me. He was reading what looked like a comic book and I asked him what it was. He closed the comic and showed me the front cover. *The Truth About Secular Humanism*.

I said, "I've heard about that. Just what is secular humanism?"

"That's where . . ." he began. He closed his eyes, collecting his thoughts and choosing his words. "That's where, if you're a queer, you got the same rights as everybody else."

"I see."

"I hate queers."

Charley leaned forward to look around me. "So do I."

Tall came in and handed me my basketball. "Out of shape," he said. I watched him walk over to the coffee table.

Another convoy of members walked in. It must have been the officers, because they walked up to the front table and sat down facing us. One of them was Mr. Douglas, my English teacher.

He was looking sideways from me and I thought I might be able to slip out the door. I walked toward it. My pal Shorty spotted me and said, "Hey, Chris. You ain't leaving, are you?"

"Well, yeah." I continued slowly toward the door. Mr. Douglas was still turned away, talking to a guy on his right. "I think I better." I got to the door and Mr. Douglas looked up. His mouth started to form a question. I said, "Because if you guys don't like Ray Charles"—I found the doorknob and turned it—"you can all just kiss my ass."

It was dark outside. I took a few steps before the door opened behind me and Mr. Douglas yelled, "Hey. Wait up, you."

I turned around and he walked up to me, real close, without slowing down. "What the hell are you doing here?"

"Nothing," I said. It was such a great comeback that I repeated it. "Nothing." I backed off a step and he closed the distance between us.

"What do you think you're up to, huh?" He pushed me backward. "Someone was in Mrs. Holder's house." He pushed me again. "Cleaned out Ben's desk." Another push. "Left a sack on the kitchen table." Another push. "That was you, wasn't it?"

"Don't push me again."

"Oh, yeah?" I had my basketball against my chest and Mr. Douglas shoved against it. I fell against the back of Shorty's pickup. "Tell me what you're up to." His face was right in mine. His breath was hot and damp against my forehead. I turned my head and saw Stienert walking up between two cars. I looked back to Mr. Douglas and smiled at him. It made him step back. I said, "What are you going to do, tough guy?"

Mr. Douglas said, "I'll tell you what I'm going to do, you little fart."

I didn't see the knife. I just felt a pressure against the basketball and heard the air hissing out.

Mr. Douglas jerked the knife free and held it up where I could see it, turning it in his hand so that the blade reflected light from the streetlamps. He talked slowly with his teeth together. "I'm going to cut your fucking nuts off."

Stienert came up behind Douglas and pressed the barrel of his gun against his neck. Mr. Douglas's eyes opened very wide.

"Who this dude, Little Moon?"

"You should be able to guess, Moon. My English teacher."

"Quality of education going to the dogs," Stienert said. "Let's drop the knife, teach."

The knife clattered to the pavement. Stienert said, "Spread 'em, teach. Put your hands on the truck."

I moved aside and Stienert performed a quick one-handed search. Mr. Douglas turned his head to look at Stienert. He said, "I should have known. A spade."

"A detective spade," Stienert said. He reached into his pocket, took out some keys, and handed them to me. "Open my trunk, Chris. Bring them both."

Stienert's car was two cars away. I heard Mr. Douglas say, "What're you going to do, darky?"

"Arrest your ass, teach. Assault with a deadly weapon, possession of a switchblade, malicious destruction. Call me some more clever names, I think of something else."

I opened the trunk. There were two shotguns inside fastened to metal clips. I put my ball in the trunk and jerked the shotguns free.

Mr. Douglas said, "I've got thirty friends in there. All I got to do is holler."

"Don't do it, teach. Wouldn't be a fair fight, only thirty

rednecks against ol' Chris and me." Stienert took his gun
away from Mr. Douglas's neck and I handed him a shotgun.
He put the pistol in a hip holster and pumped a shell into the
chamber. "You do it too, Little Moon."

I worked the pump. Stienert said, "Okay, teach. Turn
around."

Douglas looked at the shotguns.

"You can yell now," Stienert said. "Call your friends."

Mr. Douglas shook his head.

Stienert showed his teeth. "Come on. Yell."

Douglas shook his head again and Stienert pointed to the
car with his shotgun. "In the back." Mr. Douglas climbed in
the backseat. Stienert reached through the driver's side window and pressed a button. I heard the rear locks snap. There
was a wire mesh between the front and back seats. "Jump in,
Little Moon."

I started around the car. The door to the meeting room
opened and Shorty peeked his head out. Stienert fired his
shotgun in the air and Shorty's head went back inside.

On the way to the police station I told Stienert what had
happened at the meeting.

"You really say that?" he asked. "You really say, 'If you-all
don't like Ray Charles, then kiss my ass'?"

"Something like that."

Stienert slapped his knee. "You really something, Little
Moon. You really something, you know that? Glad I didn't
let ol' teach here cut your balls off."

"You should have stayed out of it," I said. "I was just
getting ready to beat the hell out of him."

"Shee-it, man." Stienert adjusted the rearview mirror to
look at Mr. Douglas. "Hear that, teach? I rescue your ass."

Mr. Douglas said, "Fuck you."

"Clever repartee, teach." Stienert poked me in the side.
"Ain't it something the way good breeding always shows?"

"Caucasian superiority," I said.

"Yeah. Jeez, I'm having a good time."

"Me too. Thanks. Thanks for coming."

We pulled into the police underground parking. "We book ol' teach here and you have to give a statement."

"Okay."

"You press charges?"

"If you want me to."

"Then we let Baker question him. Baker in a bad mood anyway. Pissed 'cause he didn't catch Mote. He have a good time with ol' teach. Then you and me go eat something."

"Okay."

Stienert pulled into a parking slot. He turned off the ignition and sat there humming to himself. "Make a good title," he said. "Make a good title of a country song or some blues." He hummed some more, patting the dashboard and swaying his head the way Stevie Wonder does. He sang the words in a high falsetto; " 'Cause if you don't like Ray Charles, just kiss my ass." He slapped me on the leg and said, "Let's go."

▲ 13 ▲

NOBODY SEEMED to be having a good time at police headquarters. I ended up sitting in a small room off a hallway. Someone had thrown up in the room earlier and the smell battled with the odor of disinfectant. The vomit smell was winning.

A policewoman came in and sat behind a dictation typewriter. She must have been twenty pounds lighter when she first joined the police force and got fitted for her uniform. Her nametag said Sgt. Canzano, and she had a fine-grained black mustache. She asked me my name, address, age, and social security number.

I said, "I don't have my card and I can't remember the number."

She said, "Gotta drabin labin?"

"Ma'am?"

"A drabin labin. It's on your drabin labin."

I said, "I don't know what a drabin labin is."

"You draba motor vehicle?"

"Yes, ma'am. Sometimes."

"Then you gotta have a drabin labin."

"Oh." I gave her a winning smile and she sighed and rolled her eyes. I read the number off my driver's license.

"Namadaccused?"

"I beg your pardon?"

"Namadaccused, namadaccused."

"Oh, Douglas. Mr. Douglas. I don't know his first name."

"Timadaincident?"

"About seven-thirty tonight."

"Okay, wadappened?"

I told her what happened. She kept right up with me on the dictation machine.

"Did the accused actually threaten bodily harm?" She said it very clearly and I understood every word.

"Yes, ma'am."

"How's that?"

"Well, he had this knife and he threatened to cut off . . . he said he was going to cut off a portion of my body."

"What portion?"

"Ah, my, ah, testicles."

"Atwadhe said? *Testicles?*"

"He might have said *balls.* I'm not sure. It was either *balls* or *nuts.*"

"Make up your mind."

"I think it was *nuts.* In fact, I'm sure it was *nuts. Fucking nuts,* to be exact."

She typed some more and almost smiled. Then she tore out the paper, turned off the machine, and went out the door. Maybe she smiled out in the hall where no one could see her.

I sat there and tried to think of something besides the smells. In ten minutes Sergeant Canzano came back with Detective Stienert. He told me to read the typewritten statement and sign it if it was accurate. I began reading it over.

The policewoman hiked a hip up on the table and lit a cigarette. She told Stienert, "Boy here was afraid to say *nuts* in front of me. Had to coax it out of him."

Stienert said, "He cultured."

I signed the sheet and they both witnessed my signature. As we left the room the policewoman said, "See you, kid," and slapped my behind like a baseball player.

We went down a stairwell. Stienert said, "You like ribs?"

"Yes, I like them a lot."

Stienert opened the door. "Vicki say to tell you hi."

"You talked to Vicki?"

"Uh-huh. She made me promise to call, let her know you safe and sound." Stienert gave me a broad smile. "Vicki think you're hot stuff."

I said, "She cultured, Mr. Stienert."

"Call me Ed," he said. "Ed, or Moon."

Stienert was driving down back streets, turning every few blocks. I said, "I'm just now starting to get scared."

"Okay to be scared. Just so you don't act scared." He came to a dead-end street and had to back up and turn around.

I said, "How come you always stay on back streets?"

"Looking for somebody." He drove down some more side streets, never getting over fifteen miles an hour. I said, "How about the VW in the pictures? Did you find out the license number?"

"No, just the first two letters, XT. Means it a local car, registered in the county. About fifty VWs in the county."

"Have you got a list of them?"

"Uh-huh."

"Could I see it?"

"What for?"

"Maybe I'd recognize a name."

We had to stop at a railroad crossing. The freight train rolled past doing paradiddles on a loose tie. Stienert said, "Yeah, I guess you can look at it. Don't want you chasing off after somebody though. Don't want you to get in trouble again." He opened the glove compartment and took out four or five thick manila envelopes. He sorted through them and dropped one on the seat. It said Holder on the front.

The train was slowing down. Stienert put the gear shift into Park and turned toward me, his arm on the back of the seat. "We have to talk about something, Little Moon."

"About what?"

"About you and me." The train had slowed to a stop. "I told you Mote had been spotted and you went down to warn him, didn't you?"

"Yeah, I did."

"Fair enough. That was my mistake. I shouldn't have told you he'd been spotted. Somebody saw him using a pay phone. I should have guessed he had called you. That was my mistake."

I tried to figure out where this conversation was heading. Stienert said, "I told you not to go to that ERWA meeting and you went anyway. That was your mistake."

"You said they weren't violent."

"I tell you don't go."

"Yeah, but you said they weren't violent. I was just trying to help out."

"That was your mistake, Little Moon."

"They invited me in."

"Mistake, Moon. You made a mistake."

"Well, how are we going to find out who killed Holder if we don't—"

Stienert yelled, "Hey!"

I jerked around to look at him.

"I tell you not to go, right?"

"Uh-huh, but—"

"And you go anyway, right?"

"Well, I thought—"

"And you just about get cut up with a knife, huh?"

"Ah—"

"So you make a mistake or not?"

"Yeah, okay, I made a mistake."

Stienert turned back to face the windshield. The train had slowed down again. Stienert tapped on the steering wheel and began laughing softly. "Like pulling teeth," he said.

The train stopped again. Stienert said, "Funny, isn't it, the way we do when somebody tries to tell us we wrong? Right away we start denying it, get defensive." He smiled and mimicked my voice, " 'But you said they weren't violent. They invited me in.' "

I had to laugh. He did my voice pretty well.

"I did the same thing," Stienert said. "Baker chewed me out for telling you that he was going to look for Mote. Right away I get defensive. Don't do no good—the man's right."

The train gave another lurch and rolled forward. "Maybe someday you give me some tennis lessons, Little Moon."

"Sure."

"You tell me I'm doing something wrong, I don't argue with you. You tell me I hold the racket wrong, I don't deny it. You see what I getting at?"

"I think so."

"I know how people get in trouble. That's my business. Nice people get in trouble, they hang out with bad people, go where they shouldn't be. Next thing you know, they in trouble. I tell you don't go somewhere, you don't go."

"Okay, Moon. I won't."

"Okay. I won't say no more about it."

I said, "Any more."

"Yeah, yeah. I know."

The train rattled past. Stienert drove over the tracks. I said, "You sound like Mote, you know that?"

"How's that?"

"Mote said, 'Keep crazies out of your life.' He didn't give advice very often, but that's something he said several times. He just said to stay away from them, don't get involved with crazies. He said you always end up losing, always end up getting in trouble, while the crazies just go right on being crazies."

"Pretty good advice," Stienert said. On the next block were newly constructed apartment buildings. Stienert parked behind a car that had two bumper stickers on it. The one on the left said Shit Happens. The one on the right said God Rules.

Stienert noticed the stickers too. "Interesting philosophical position," he said.

I looked around. "Is there a restaurant here?"

"My fiancée lives here. Come on."

Her name was Kate and she looked like she could have modeled for the little statuettes of African art you see in museums. She was very black, slender, with small, pointed breasts. She had high, prominent buttocks and wore her hair in a short Afro that accentuated her long neck.

She and Stienert embraced. There was music playing in the background, big-band jazz. She told us to have a seat and disappeared into the kitchen. Stienert looked through the manila envelope, pulled out three sheets of paper, and handed them to me. Then he followed Kate into the kitchen

I read the names of the VW owners on the first page. It was hard to concentrate, because there were food smells and giggling sounds from the kitchen. I heard Kate say, "Stop."

I drew a blank on the second page. While I was reading over the last page Stienert and Kate sat down across from me on the sofa. No names jumped out at me from the list. I said, "Can I keep this?"

"No."

"Can I look through the rest of the envelope?"

"No."

I said, "It be police business, right?"

Stienert laughed. "Uh-huh. It be police business." He turned to Kate. "Little Moon here don't like the way I talk. Don't like it when I say *it be*."

"Good for you, Chris. I hate it when he does that."

Stienert took a sip of beer. "Kate doing a paper, Little Moon. She going for her doctorate in psychology. Paper about prejudice. She be interested in hearing about the ERWA meeting."

Kate said, "Tell me while we set the table."

I went over the events and conversations. Kate listened carefully while she placed dishes and silverware. Stienert carried in a bowl of greens, some cornbread, and a platter of ribs. When I saw the ribs my knees almost buckled. He went back to the kitchen and returned with a bowl of coleslaw and two bottles of beer. We all sat down.

Kate passed me the greens. "That is very interesting," she said. "All sorts of material there."

I took a piece of cornbread. Stienert passed me the ribs. "Eat these with your hands, Moon. Only way to eat ribs."

I took a bite of greens. It was a new flavor. "What kind of greens are these?"

"Poke," Kate said.

"Poke *salad*," Stienert said. He pronounced it *salat*. "They grows wild."

"Grow. They grow wild."

"Doing my part to preserve authentic Negro dialect. Else we all be sounding like Bryant Gumbel."

"What do you think of those men, Chris? Those men at the meeting."

The ribs were really good. I eyed the platter. Maybe Kate wouldn't eat much. "I really only talked to the one guy, Charley. He was kind of pitiful."

Kate said, "Pitiful in what way?"

"I don't know, I just felt sorry for him. He doesn't trust his daughters, for one thing. He thinks they'll get in some kind of trouble just because there's a black family next door."

Stienert said, "We irresistible to white girls."

"And he seems to be missing out on a lot. He won't watch any black shows, any black entertainers. That means he can't enjoy Bill Cosby, Eddie Murphy, Ray Charles."

"Can't watch the NBA neither," Stienert said.

Kate said, "When the short man was going to see if it was all right for you to sit in on the meeting. What made you say 'I sure do hate niggers'?"

"Seemed appropriate. Thought it would be something like the password."

"I'm sure it was appropriate. Part of the appeal of this kind of group must be the easy acceptance one gains. All that is asked is that you hate blacks and Jews and you are immediately accepted. One of the boys, so to speak."

"One of the crazies," Stienert said. He passed me some more ribs and we grinned at each other.

"There's also some evidence that racism has its roots in evolutionary history," Kate said. She took very small bites and laid her fork down while she chewed. Stienert and I had a whale of a lead on her. "Some scholars have theorized that ancient tribes survived, in part, from the proclivity to hate a common enemy and it served to tighten the tribal bond. The tendency has become genetic. They feel that we are programmed to fear and despise any group that is different from our own."

I said, "Is there horseradish in this coleslaw?"

"Yes, just a bit. And some sugar." Kate picked at the greens with her fork. "I'm boring you two, aren't I?"

I said, "No, ma'am. It's very interesting, really."

"Yes, I am, and I want to apologize. I've been working on my thesis too much lately."

Stienert said, "I'll say. Be glad when it's finished."

Kate gave Stienert a look. I put a bone in the bowl. There were two sections of ribs left and Stienert and Kate had stopped eating.

Kate said, "Please, Chris. Finish off the ribs. I'll just have to throw them away."

I was pretty sure she was going to say that. It was the best thing she had said so far.

Stienert said, "Little Moon told me something tonight. He told me about this friend of his that gave him some advice. Told him to keep crazies out of his life."

Kate said, "That's excellent advice."

I put my bone in the bowl. "Are you sure nobody wants these last ribs?"

Stienert said, "Go ahead, Moon, finish them off." Perfect.

I took a big bite. Stienert pointed his finger at Kate. "That's what's been the matter with you lately. You studying all this racism, prejudice stuff, and taking it too seriously."

"It is serious, Ed."

"What it is, is a bunch of crazies and you're trying to make sense out of it. It don't make sense. You keep thinking about it, it make *you* crazy."

"Ed, I am just . . ." She glanced at me, then looked at Stienert and smiled. "You two like each other, don't you?"

Stienert said, "A little bit."

I said, "Some."

Stienert looked at his watch. "It be getting late."

I looked at Kate. "I guess we be leaving."

We all stood up and Kate gave me a polite handshake, then a very nice cheek-to-cheek hug. Her skin was smooth and cool.

Stienert did his back-street number again, creeping along at walking speed. I said, "Who are you looking for, Moon?"

"Guy I saw a year ago. Saw him running out of a house where he raped an old lady. Didn't catch him. I get him next time."

"I thought you just worked on murder cases."

"This on my own time. Kinda personal. Don't like it he got away. Don't like it he took a shot at me either."

"So you've been driving around like this for a year?"

"Uh-huh. He's hit two different neighborhoods. Keeps going back to the same two. This one of them. Going to kill somebody sooner or later, carrying that gun."

He made another slow turn. "How you get your scar?"

"A fall. I fell down some steps, like a fire escape, when I was about one year old. How did you get yours?"

"Street fight," he said. "Boy had a big ring and a left hook. It ever bother you, your scar?"

"It used to. It used to kind of twitch and pull at my eye when I got nervous. Mote fixed that."

"How'd he do that?"

"Mote told me that our mind remembers everything but that it shuts off certain memories, especially memories where you get hurt or go through some pain. He said that's probably why my eye twitched like that. The memory was trying to get through."

Stienert turned down an alleyway between the backs of apartment buildings. "So you remembered it, huh, just like that?"

"No, it took a while. Mote told me to think about it before I went to sleep, just think real hard about the scar, and see if I had any dreams about it. That's the way it got started."

He made a slow right turn at the end of the alley. "Tell me about it."

"Well, it was a short dream, more like a short scene. I am real small and looking at the back of somebody's legs. That was all, but I knew it had something to do with my scar. I told Mote about the dream and it was really neat the way he did it, Moon. He got me to remember the whole thing."

"How did he do that, get you to remember?"

"Questions," I said. "He just kept asking me questions, like 'How big were you?, Was it daytime or nighttime?, Was it hot or cold?, What color were the legs?' And I remembered that it was pants legs and the pants were tan. Then I could see the creases in the pants, then the shoes—brown shoes with black heels. Mote would ask some more questions. 'How did you get there?, What did you smell?,' things like that. When I got stuck he would go back to the pants legs and start again, and I would remember a little more, then a little more. After a while I ended up remembering the whole thing."

"What was it?"

"Dad had gone outside on the landing in this apartment we used to live in. I followed him out. He didn't know I was there, and just when I was ready to grab hold of his legs, he turned and knocked me down a fire escape. I remembered that part too, sailing through the air, then a pain under my eye. I had cut it on some sharp piece of metal from the stairs. I remembered it all and the neat thing was that after that my eye didn't bother me anymore. It hasn't twitched or anything since."

"Mote a pretty good friend, huh? Maybe he think he doing you a favor killing Holder."

"No, when I saw Mote down at the river he said he didn't do it. It was somebody else, Moon."

"You sure?"

"Yeah, I'm sure."

"How come? How come you sure?"

"I don't know, I just am. Mote wouldn't lie to me."

"How you know that?"

"I just know. There are some people, not many, but some people that you know wouldn't lie to you. Mote's that way. If it means anything, I think you're that way too. I don't think you'd lie to me either."

Stienert said, "Hmm." He came to an intersection, turned onto a main street, and speeded up toward my house.

▲ *14* ▲

THE SUN WOKE me, blasting into my eyelids through the window. A robin was letting me have it from the backyard. I turned away from the window, onto my right side. "Shut up." I would have made it back to sleep, but the phone rang.

"Chris, are you all right?"

"Yeah, Mom. I'm fine."

"It's all over the papers and the morning news. Everybody's talking about it."

"About what?"

"About you. About you being attacked last night."

"Oh."

"I felt so stupid. Everyone asking me questions and I didn't know anything about it. You should tell me about those things."

"I'm sorry, Mom. It was late and you were in bed."

"Everybody at the office knew all about it. I didn't know what to say."

My brain started to wake up, remembering the night before.

"Chris?"

"Yes, ma'am?"

"What happened? What should I tell my friends?"

"I don't know, Mom. I just woke up. Just tell them that I'm okay and that you've got everything under control."

I hung up and was about three breaths away from going back to sleep, when the phone rang again.

"Christopher Miller, please."

"Speaking."

"Christopher, this is Mr. Reeves."

He had always called me Chris in the past. "Yes, sir."

"Would you come to my office right away, Christopher? I want to see if we can get some matters cleared up."

"At school?"

"Yes. Right away."

"Well, it will take me a little while. I just woke up and have to shower and get dressed."

He didn't say anything.

"Mr. Reeves?"

"Yes?"

"I said it will—"

"Yes, I heard you, Christopher. It is in your best interest to be as fast as possible."

"Can you tell me what this is about?"

"We'll discuss that when you get here."

"Who is *we*?"

"Mr. Douglas is here, and some other gentlemen."

"What other gentlemen?"

He said, "I'll expect you within the hour, Christopher."

The hot water felt good, beating down on my head. Life had been so much simpler just a few days ago. Brushing my teeth helped some more. *What other gentlemen?*

I called my father's office and his receptionist told me he was out. I thought about calling Mom and asking her to go with me but decided not to. I dialed police headquarters and asked for Detective Stienert. He wasn't in. "How about Lieutenant Baker?"

After a moment he picked up and said, "Baker."

I asked Baker if he would do me a favor and go to school with me to meet with the principal.

"What's it about?"

"He wouldn't say. But Mr. Douglas is there with some other guys, and I'd sure feel better if you were there."

"What do they want?"

"I don't know, Lieutenant, but last night what Mr. Douglas wanted was to stick his knife in me."

"You scared, kid?"

"No, it's just . . . Yeah, I guess you could say I'm scared."

Baker sounded grouchy. "I'll come by and get you."

He was there before I could finish dressing. I jumped in the car, buttoning my shirt while he drove. Baker wasn't wearing his wig. He didn't say anything and neither did I.

The school was clean and quiet. Baker had metal plates on his heels and his footsteps clicked and echoed around the empty halls. I opened the door to the principal's office. Miss Cavendish was still typing away. She looked at me over her glasses, then at Baker. "They're expecting you," she said.

Baker opened the door without knocking and I went in first. Mr. Reeves was behind his desk. Mr. Douglas and Shorty were sitting behind him, another guy was sitting in front of the desk.

Mr. Douglas said, "What's he doing here?" He nodded toward Baker.

I said, "I asked him to come."

"What for?"

Baker said, "I'm his career adviser."

Mr. Douglas's face was already flushed. "No, he's not," he told Mr. Reeves. "He's a policeman."

Baker said, "That's right. That means I got one of these." He pulled back his jacket and pointed to the gun in his hip holster. "You try to stab anybody, I'm going to shoot this at you."

"Let's not have any of that," Mr. Reeves said. "We're just here to get a few matters cleared up."

Baker leaned back against the door and crossed his arms. I didn't know what to do with my hands, so I stuck them in my pockets. Mr. Reeves pressed his palms together, forefingers against his lips. "I'm having trouble believing the things these gentlemen are saying about you, Christopher."

"How's that, sir?"

He took off his glasses and tapped the earpiece against his

teeth. "You've been a good student. You never got into any trouble. Suddenly you're hitting teachers, getting involved in murders, disturbing these men who were trying to have a peaceful meeting, accusing Mr. Douglas of assault."

Baker said, "It so happens he's got a good witness on that last one."

Mr. Reeves said, "Let's let the boy talk for himself. What do you say to these charges, Christopher?"

"What charges, sir?"

The guy in the chair said, "Breaking up a peaceful political meeting. Interfering with the right to free assembly."

Baker said, "You don't make charges at a high school principal's office. You go down to headquarters to do that."

I said, "I didn't mean to break up the meeting, Mr. Reeves."

"I understand you shouted a vulgar insult to the membership, then ran out the door. Is that true, Christopher?"

"Yes, sir, that's true. I mean, it's kind of true. It wasn't as bad as you made it sound."

"Well, what have you got to say for yourself?"

I said, "Ah, gee, Mr. Reeves, I don't know." I was getting that sting-y feeling in back of my eyes. I didn't want to cry in front of this bunch. "Like Lieutenant Baker here says, if you guys want to go down there and tell the police that I told you to kiss my ass, I'll go with you and plead guilty."

"No one is talking about reporting you to the police," Mr. Reeves said.

Mr. Douglas said, "Not yet anyway." He looked me in the eyes.

No one else was looking at me and I mouthed the words Kiss my ass at him.

Mr. Douglas stood up and said, "You little cocksucker."

Baker said, "There's your countercharge, kid. *You cocksucker* carries more weight than *kiss my ass*."

Mr. Reeves slapped his hand on his desk. "Gentlemen, please!" he shouted. "I will not tolerate this kind of language in my office." He turned to Mr. Douglas. "Especially from you."

Mr. Douglas sputtered something and pointed at me. Mr. Reeves told him to be quiet. "Now, everybody calm down. This will be a peaceful, orderly meeting." He ran his fingers through his hair, then picked up some papers from his desk. "I have your English examination here, Christopher. Mr. Douglas feels that you had the test questions before the examination. He thinks that you might have entered Mr. Holder's house to steal them."

"That's not true, Mr. Reeves."

He looked at the papers. "How do you explain your grade? You got every one of the answers correct, and your essay on Steinbeck makes one suspicious that it was prepared in advance."

"I knew that stuff, that's all. I like Steinbeck, he's one of my favorite writers."

Baker said, "Who's Lennie?"

"You mean Steinbeck's Lennie?"

"Yeah."

"He's the dumb guy in *Of Mice and Men*. You like Steinbeck?"

"Uh-huh. Who's Charley?"

"A black French poodle."

"Hazel?"

"The big dumb guy from *Cannery Row* and *Sweet Thursday*."

Baker looked at Douglas. "Did you know that?"

"Of course."

Mr. Reeves said, "I didn't." He turned around and looked at Mr. Douglas. Then he turned and looked at the guy in the chair and nodded. The guy got out of the chair and stood facing me.

"Tell you what, Chris." He smiled. "Okay I call you Chris?"

"Sure."

"My name is Ken Allison. I'm an attorney." He was a big guy with a square jaw and black-rimmed glasses. He looked like Clark Kent. He tilted his head and looked me over. "What do you say we just forget the whole thing?"

"What whole thing?"

"This whole mess." He waved his arm in a gesture that took in the entire room. "You drop the charges against Mr. Douglas and we'll forget about you disturbing the peace, interfering with the right to free assembly, inciting to riot, cheating on exams." He put his hand on my shoulder and smiled. "What do you say?"

Baker said, "Don't do it, kid."

I thought it over, looked at Mr. Douglas, Shorty, and Mr. Reeves. Then I held out my hand and Clark Kent took it. While we were shaking hands I smiled at him and said, "Kiss my ass."

He jerked his hand away. Baker said, "Let's go, kid."

We walked out the door quickly, too quickly for Miss Cavendish. She was slumped down in her chair, laughing silently into a handkerchief. She turned off the intercom and sat up very straight. Then she burst out laughing again and waved us away with her handkerchief.

We walked down the empty hallway. Baker stopped and opened the door to the auditorium and looked in. I waited for him. He stared into the room for a minute before he closed the door. "Hasn't changed much," he said.

"You went to school here?"

"Uh-huh. Class of '65. Good school back then."

"It still is," I said.

Baker pointed to a classroom, "Algebra. Boy, I hated algebra. Never could figure out why you had to add up letters."

I wanted to explain it, but I didn't understand either.

We got in the car. Baker said, "You want some breakfast, some coffee or something?"

"Sure."

"Have you heard from Thomas, talked to him anymore?"

"No. What happened with the dogs?"

Baker said, "Lost him. Just a matter of time though." He spoke into his radio mike and the voice that answered was unintelligible. He returned the mike to a hook.

"Aren't you supposed to say ten four or something?"

"If you talk to him, if you see him or he calls, ask him if he'd take a lie-detector test."

"What would happen?" I said. "What would happen if he took the test and passed?"

Baker pulled into a restaurant parking lot. "It'd be in his favor. Make his story more believable."

The cashier smiled at Baker and said, "Hi, Frank." The restaurant was empty and we took a table. A waitress brought over two coffees.

"If he passed the lie-detector test, would you let him go?"

"No. Still have to hold him." Baker took a sip of coffee.

I said, "Don't you want some sugar?"

Baker shook his head.

"At our house, when you and Stienert came to question us, you took a lot of sugar."

Baker shrugged his shoulders and picked up a menu.

"What's that mean?" I said. I mimicked Baker's shrug.

"Doesn't mean anything."

We each ordered bacon and eggs.

I said, "I've got a hunch that you and Stienert were doing a number on us that first night."

Baker shrugged again. He looked around the restaurant.

"Were you?"

"Yeah, maybe. Usually Ed plays the mean, dumb cop and I play the nice guy. Sometimes we switch and I do the dumb guy."

I said, "You do it very well."

Baker laughed. It was the first time I heard him laugh. "Lots of natural ability. Our senior year we put on *Of Mice and Men* and I played Lennie."

"Is that what got you interested in Steinbeck?"

"Yeah."

I said, "What else do you read, besides Steinbeck?"

He shrugged again. "This and that." He loosened his collar.

I said, "If Mote calls, I'll ask him about the lie-detector business, but I don't think he'll come in. I think something happened in 'Nam that . . . I don't think he wants to be locked up."

Baker nodded. "You ask him anyway."

I said, "Don't get sore, Lieutenant, but I think you look a lot better without the hairpiece."

He rubbed his hand over his bald spot. "Me too. The wife likes it. Says it will even stay on while you're swimming."

"You do a lot of swimming?"

"No, never learned to swim."

The waitress refilled our cups. I said, "I appreciate you coming with me, Lieutenant. Those guys would have really intimidated me if you hadn't been there."

Baker nodded. He took a wad of money out of his pocket and laid a five on the table. "You ready to go?"

"Yes, sir."

We went out the door. Baker said, "You know how to box, kid? You know karate or anything?"

"No, why?"

"You should. You go around being a tough guy and telling people to kiss your ass. You should have something to back up your sass."

We got in the car. "I've got you and Stienert," I said.

"No, you don't. You got yourself, that's all. Sooner or later, all you got's yourself."

We drove off. Baker said, "If you were five years older, a few pounds heavier, I'd of popped you a couple of times already."

"Why?"

Baker shrugged. "You just need poppin', that's all. Too big for your britches. You think you're smarter than everybody else. Maybe you are, but you ought to keep it to yourself. Don't be so full of yourself, like you got it all figured out."

"I don't have it all figured out."

"Damned right you don't."

I SAW BILLY'S car in their driveway and went straight to his house, opened the door, and yelled, "Hello."

"In the kitchen, Chris."

Billy and his mom were unpacking groceries. I said, "How was grandma's?"

"Great, really fun. What's been happening?"

"Lots. Lots has happened, all kinds of stuff."

Billy's mom said that she would put the rest of the groceries away and we went out on the porch. I told Billy about Husky Voice's call and about playing tennis with Sweeny and Husky Voice shooting out the porch light, then calling again.

I told him about going fishing with Vicki and Stacy and meeting Mote. Then I told him about going to the ERWA meeting and Mr. Douglas's attack and police headquarters.

Billy's mom brought out two glasses of iced tea. She said, "I'm making sandwiches," and patted my cheek. I could still taste the greasy bacon and eggs, but Billy's mom liked to watch me eat, so I didn't say anything. Noble.

I told Billy about meeting Stienert's fiancée and how I had to go to school to meet with Mr. Reeves, Mr. Douglas, and the attorney. Billy's mom brought out roast-beef sandwiches on whole-wheat bread. She had put lots of onions on mine and mixed hot mustard with the mayonnaise. There were homemade pickles too.

I took a bite and all thoughts of bacon and eggs were gone. Billy's mom stood on the porch, waiting for our approval. I rolled my eyes and moaned. Billy said, "Really good, Mom."

She smiled. I said, "Will you marry me?" and she laughed like it was the funniest thing she had ever heard. She was even blushing as she went back inside.

I took another bite. "You know what would be nice, Billy?"

"What?"

"It would be nice if your mom and my mom could trade bodies for a while, a few days."

"What for?"

"I think it would be good for both of them," I said. "I mean, I think your mom would really enjoy being pretty for a few days, getting the attention and all. And I think it would help my mom if she wasn't so beautiful. She might develop a little more character."

Billy didn't say anything. I ate some pickles. Billy would think about what I'd said for a few days, then have a good comment. I finished my sandwich. "Here's what we have to do, Billy. We have to figure out who else knew the combination to our lock."

"Why?"

"Remember when the cops came that first night? They had to break the lock to get into our shack. Mote said he'd locked up before he left. That means someone had to unlock it, take one of Mote's knives, lock the door back up, and kill Holder."

Billy said, "You don't think Leon did it, do you?"

"No. Leon couldn't keep something like that secret. But who else knew the combination?"

"Let's go talk to Leon."

When we got to Leon's house Willa answered the door, wearing a T-shirt and no brassiere. She had on brief shorts and the T-shirt was too small for her. Looking at her was like taking a hit in the stomach.

I said, "Wow," and covered my eyes with my palms. Willa

smiled. Mote had said that he thought most girls didn't realize the power their bodies had over men, but I think Willa did. It was that kind of smile.

Billy said, "Is Leon around?"

Willa shook her head. "Just me and Grandma."

I said, "Did Leon ever give anyone the combination to our lock on the clubhouse?"

"No. He acted like it was a big secret thing." She leaned against the door and examined her fingernails.

I said, "Willa, who told you about the petition that Holder was taking around?"

"How you know about that?"

"Leon told me. I forced it out of him."

"I found out from Mrs. Crowly," Willa said. "Mrs. Crowly told me that Mr. Holder came around with a paper that some lawyer had made up. It said that Leon was mentally in-incom—"

"Incompetent?"

"Yeah. It said he was like that and should be in an institution. She said there was a lot of names on it."

"Did she tell you any names?"

Willa shook her head. "Uh-uh. She just wanted to warn us. Wanted me to tell my father."

"Where is Leon?"

"He's over there now. He's over at Mrs. Crowly's now, helping dig some kind of ditch."

We walked back the way we had come. Mrs. Crowly lived next to my house, on the other side from Billy. Billy said, "What are you smiling about?"

"Mrs. Crowly. The things she says."

"She drives me nuts."

"Me too, but she does great dialogue and Mote said I was lucky to have her next door."

"He did? When did he say that?"

"A couple of years ago. Mote said he wanted to ask me something. You know how he did sometimes, act like what you had to say was the most interesting thing in the world.

This was one of those times, like I would be doing him an enormous favor by telling him something."

Billy said, "He used to do that with me too."

"Mote's question was, when did I first realize that I was smarter than some grown-ups? I didn't have to think about it very much. I knew right away when it had happened and told Mote about it."

"When did that happen?"

"Mrs. Crowly," I said. "I was about nine years old and she had asked me into her kitchen for some cookies and milk. She was telling me about astronomy and had it all screwed up—the sun revolving around the earth, the earth rotating on its polar system. You know how she does.

"Anyway, I told Mote how I remembered sitting there eating cookies and suddenly realized that something was wrong with Mrs. Crowly's thinking, that my mind was better than hers."

Billy said, "What did Mote say about it?"

"He just said it was an important event. He talked about how some people never do that, never learn to trust their own thinking over other people's. After they grow up, he said, they still let other people tell them what to do, how to think. Like teachers, preachers, politicians, lawyers. That's why he said that I was lucky to know Mrs. Crowly."

Billy said, "She drives me nuts."

Leon and Mrs. Crowly were in the backyard. Leon was digging a trench for a wall and Mrs. Crowly was watching him. She was about forty-five years old, with big, wide hips. She wore jeans and a checkered shirt. There were about fifteen pens in her shirt pocket in a plastic liner that said Carl's Auto Parts.

We admired the trench. Leon kept right on working, looking up now and then for approval. Billy asked Mrs. Crowly about the petition and Mrs. Crowly led us toward her back door, out of Leon's hearing.

"He came around, oh, two, three weeks ago with it. I wouldn't sign it. Leon's a good boy and his family are good people, real clean colored persons."

"What did Mr. Holder say?" Billy asked.

"Oh, about how you have one family of blacks and soon the whole neighborhood is black and about Leon looking at white women." She put her hands in her hip pockets. "People have to learn they can't go making these premental judgments."

Billy said, "Premental judgments?"

"Yes. Lots of people make these premental judgments."

I said, "You ever do that, Mrs. Crowly?"

"Try not." She looked at Leon, then tilted her head for us to come closer.

I thought, Here it comes.

"This what gets me," she said. "This what makes me mad. When a momma and a daddy won't admit that they hadn't made their kids mind and they got one of them that . . . She likes to go out here, and I mean, it's okay for the whites to mix and things, low incomes, and mess around but"—she leaned toward us and whispered—"no blacks."

She rocked back on her heels and pursed her lips. I glanced at Billy. Mrs. Crowly said, "I'd be the best friend they ever had in the world. Call me for any kind of favor, but as far as mixing and marrying into them, I don't believe in it."

Billy said, "You think that's wrong, Mrs. Crowly?"

"Well, what's the wrong factor is the children, Billy. When the children grow up, the factor is there. They don't want . . . the blacks don't want them, the whites don't want them— and that's the worst factor. I love, you know, I love people. Do anything in the world for people, but I don't . . . no premental judgments."

Billy said, "I wish more people were like you, Mrs. Crowly."

I said, "It would be a far better world."

Mrs. Crowly said, "Would you boys like a Coke?"

We said we would. Mrs. Crowly went into her house. Billy said, "Can you remember all that?"

"I'm going to try. I want to write it down, tape it to my bathroom mirror, so I can read it every morning."

Mrs. Crowly came out with a tray, glasses filled with ice

and a half-gallon bottle of Coke. She hollered Leon over and poured the drinks. "This is the old Coke," she said. "I don't like that new Coke. The old Coke's better."

Billy said, "You're right."

Mrs. Crowly said, "Worst mistake they ever made, that new Coke. Too sweet. I told them, this new Coke is too sweet."

Leon came over and we all sat on the back steps with our drinks. Leon's glasses were crooked and I straightened them.

I said, "Mrs. Crowly, there's something I've been wanting to ask you about. I'd like your opinion on something."

"What's that, Chris?"

"Well, you hear a lot about evolution nowadays. I just wondered if you knew what it was."

"What that means is the zoo, the zoo, goo, you."

"Say what?" Billy asked.

"That the sea . . . is the goo in the sea?"

"Yeah."

"To you, Z, the goo, to the zoo, the monkey, to you."

Billy looked at me, puzzled.

I said, "From the goo, to the zoo, to you. Is that it?"

"Yeah," Mrs. Crowly said. "They say—the evolutionists say—somebody slung something out, it hit the water and it become a puddle, and in two, three weeks it expanded on out and become a snake, a snail, to a this. I don't believe that stuff."

I said, "I think they say it took more than a few weeks though."

"One guy said it took six million years." She repeated it, "six million years," and laughed. "Didn't take no six million years."

Leon was taking all this in. He finished his Coke and went back to work. I laid down my glass and walked over to him. He was swinging an ax, cutting through some tree roots. "Leon, did you ever tell anyone the combination to our lock?"

He laid down the ax and picked up the shovel. "Uh-uh, I

never told anybody." He scooped some loose dirt out of the trench. "Still got it right here." He pulled off his hat and handed it to me. The combination was written on the inside.

I said, "What are you going to do with the dirt, Leon?"

"I don't know. Mrs. Crowly didn't tell me."

I said, "Maybe you could dig a hole and bury it."

Leon said, "Uh-huh. Whatever Mrs. Crowly says." He shoveled out some loose dirt, then leaned on the handle. "You can't put dirt in a hole, Chris."

"Why not."

"Because you'd still have dirt left over."

"What if you stamped it down real hard?"

"No," he said. "Your trouble is you read too many books."

Billy and I walked back toward our houses. "Mrs. Crowly votes," Billy said.

"Yeah. Scary, huh?"

"What do we do next, Chris?"

"I don't know. I don't know what to do."

"Me neither."

We walked along without talking for a block. "We've been getting bad moves, Billy."

"Huh?"

"Bad moves. You know, the Big Guy in the Sky who is moving us around, spinning the wheel. We have been getting all the bad moves and spins. Maybe we'll get a better one soon."

Billy said, "Or we could get another bad one."

▲ *16* ▲

HE WORE a blue cord summer-weight suit, a gray checked hat, and a stocking mask. There was a long-barreled pistol in his right hand and I knew it was Husky Voice before he spoke.

I sat on the edge of my bed and looked at him standing in the doorway of my bedroom. He had something in his left hand with black leather straps on it. He tossed it at me and I caught it. He said, "Put that on, John."

It looked like a small transistor radio attached to a short, thick belt. "What is this?"

He pointed the gun at my forehead. The hole in the barrel looked huge. "Put it on, Ron."

I looked down at the device in my lap.

"Around your neck." It was a hoarse whisper that made me want to clear my throat. I put on the collar. The leather was stiff and my hands were shaking, but I got it fastened.

"Button the shirt, Burt."

I worked with the buttons. "What is this thing?"

He put the gun under his jacket and pulled out what looked like another transistor radio from his pocket. An electric shock hit me in the neck. It shuddered up and down my spine and out both arms for about three seconds. I would have screamed, but I didn't have any breath to do it with.

He said, "Bad, ain't it, lad?"

I nodded yes and felt the collar.

"Fresh batteries," he said. "Those new alkaline jobs." He leaned against the doorway. "Tell me where the ledger is, we take off the collar, and I go away, Jay."

"Mister, I don't know anything about—"

He pressed the button again. A short burst this time and when he stopped, the muscles along my upper back kept jumping by themselves.

"Jesus, please don't do that again. Please."

"The book, where's the book?"

My teeth were chattering. I shook my head. "I wish I knew where it was. Listen, don't shock me again. Let me tell you the truth." My breath was coming in jerky sobs. I told him about waiting outside Holder's house, watching Mrs. Holder and Mr. Douglas leave together, then going in the back door. I told him about hearing someone come in while I hid upstairs. "They must have done it. They must have taken the book. The only other possibility I can think of is that Mr. Douglas took it."

"Who's Douglas?"

"My English teacher. He was in ERWA with Mr. Holder."

"I read in the paper that you went to that meeting." He stopped for a breath. "You went there to sell them the ledger, didn't you?"

"No. I don't—"

Husky Voice said, "Lie on the bed, Fred."

I lay back on the bed. Husky Voice dialed the phone by my bedside. His breath rasped all the time. When someone answered he said, "Does the name Douglas mean anything to you?"

I could hear some conversation from the receiver. Husky Voice looked around while he listened. He saw the five hundred-dollar bills on my dresser and stuffed them into his pocket.

"The kid says Douglas was at the house before he went in." He listened to the reply while he looked at me. I couldn't make out any of his features from under the nylon. While the other person talked, Husky Voice shook his head back and forth at me. He said, "I'll get back to you. About an hour, sunflower."

He hung up. "Let's take a ride, Clyde." He made a lifting motion with his hand. He had on rubber gloves.

I sat up and reached for my shoes. "Uh-uh, leave the shoes.'" He waved for me to stand up. "We'll walk out to the car. Don't try to run. This thing's got a long range."

I stood up and headed for the door. Husky Voice stayed about five feet behind me. "Blue car," he said. "Parked at the curb, Herb."

I walked out the front door. No traffic, no friends or neighbors in sight. There was a blue sedan across the street. Husky Voice whispered. "Front seat, Pete."

I got in the front seat. The car was clean and new. He started the car and said, "Bend over, Rover. Put your head between your knees." I hesitated, just a second, and he gave me a short burst with his shocker. "Hands behind your head, Ted."

He drove about two blocks and turned right. I said, "Where we going?" and he shocked me again. My head jerked back and hit the bottom of the dashboard. It made a metallic taste in my mouth, copper.

He drove for about five minutes. My heart was beating like crazy. He stopped and switched off the engine. He opened his door. "Keep your head down low, Joe."

The door opened on my side. He said, "Look between your feet, Pete."

I looked. There was a shopping bag on the floor.

"Put it over your head, Jed."

I was doing everything he asked.

"Out."

I got out. He bunched up the back of my shirt with his fist and pushed. I put my hands in front of me, feeling space. We climbed steps and I felt carpeting with my bare feet. He pushed me to the right, his hand bunched in my shirt again. Then we turned left and walked a few steps. "Stop. Turn around."

I turned and he pushed me backward. I fell across a bed. He grabbed my foot and pulled. "Down this way." I scooted down, heels and elbows. "Okay, lie still, straighten your legs and lie still, Bill." He was breathing hard.

When I straightened my legs they hung over the end of the bed, the footboard striking me just above the ankles. I listened to him move around the room, opening drawers and sucking air in and out. When he touched me I jerked. He was wrapping something around my left ankle, pressing down against the footrail with one hand, wrapping with the other. I smelled the adhesive tape. He did the other ankle. I was shivering.

"Sit up. Take off the sack, Jack."

We were in a bedroom. A video camera was set up at the foot of the bed on a tripod, and Husky Voice was aiming it at my face. He pushed a button and a small red light came on.

"Look at the camera."

I looked at the camera and around the room. It was a very ordinary room. Full-length drapes covered the windows.

"Pull up your trousers."

"What for?"

The shock made me jerk back down on the bed and bridge up on the back of my neck.

Husky Voice came around to the side of the bed and looked down on me. He had a paddle in his right hand, the kind that college fraternities use. "Gotta make sure, kid. My people still think you know something. They want some proof."

"I don't. I swear I don't know anything else. I told you everything. Don't hurt me."

He nodded. "I believe you. They don't"—he pointed at the camera—"so we got to break some bones, Jones." He raised the paddle and brought it down across both shins sideways.

I screamed and sat up.

He swung from the side.

The paddle hit me flat in the face. I tasted blood and my

nose filled up with it. It didn't do any good to squirm, but I squirmed anyway.

He smacked the bottom of my feet.

I watched him do it, unable to sit up or jerk away.

He took lumberjack swings. When he stopped, he was barely able to get his breath and had to bend over and rest a moment before he said, "Sit up."

I sat up. Blood ripped down the back of my throat and I gagged, swallowed, then vomited. I tried to catch it in my hands, but it spilled over onto my clothes and the bed.

Husky Voice grabbed my hair and jerked my head up to face the camera. "Where's the ledger?"

I shook my head. "I don't know."

He hit me in the face again and took several more whacks on my shins.

I tried to sit up and grab him but passed out.

It was like going down a whirlpool, spinning and turning and tumbling in lazy slow motion. Pain had stopped. I came to the bottom of the pool and lay there. Maybe it was minutes, maybe it was a few seconds. Then I started to spiral back up. I wanted to stay down, but something was pulling me, tugging me back toward consciousness. It was the pain.

Husky Voice was talking. ". . . and I got it all on tape. You can see for yourself. He don't know. He don't know shit."

I lay still. The pain was bad everywhere, but I knew it would be worse if I moved. Husky Voice spoke into the phone again. "It don't matter. Everything went smooth. Nobody saw us leave. I can drop him somewhere or whatever you want."

Silence.

"Your money, honey. Cost you an extra thousand. Either way you say, Kay."

I opened my eyes a slit. Husky had his back to me. He had the phone in one hand and was pulling back the drape to look out the window. "Yeah, uh-huh. Nah, I'm going back home unless you can think of something else, somebody else who could have took it. Otherwise I'm flying out tonight."

He started to turn and I shut my eyes.

"He's still out. Broke up his tibias some, I think."

He listened.

"Tibias. The shinbones. The boy's in shock, Doc."

I could tell by his voice that he had turned away again. I peeked out of slit eyes. He was looking out the window, holding the drape open. "About two hours. I'll wait till it gets dark."

He reached into his pocket and pulled out the transmitter. "Yeah, see you at your place. Have the thousand ready, Eddie." He hung up the phone and began to turn. I knew it was coming. The shock wrenched my neck back against my shoulderblades, shot down my spine and my arms, but I kept my eyes closed. Husky Voice breathed on by and went past the bed. I heard water running and opened my eyes.

The paddle was on the bed. The front of my shirt was bloody. I tried to sit up but didn't make it. I was about to try again, when I heard the water stop running. Husky Voice came wheezing back into the bedroom. He stopped by the bed and I felt him looking at me. I wanted to swallow.

He cut the tape that fastened my ankles to the bedrail. I felt a rush as blood hit my feet and set them on fire. He put my feet together and started wrapping the ankles. I grabbed the paddle with both hands and swung it sideways with everything I had left. The edge of the paddle caught him on the temple, dead solid. My follow-through splintered off the top of the bedpost.

He had been leaning over me, taping my feet, and fell half sideways. His chin whacked the bedrail as he went down hard on his back. I shifted around on the bed and hit him on top of the head several times. The paddle stung my hands, but I swung again and the last hit made something crack.

He lay very still. I couldn't hear him breathe and I didn't care. I hung over the edge of the bed and pulled his gun from under his coat. I pointed it at his head and thought about it.

The phone. It was across the room. I sat up and saw my legs for the first time. There were three large, blue egg-size swellings on the left leg, two on the right. My feet were swollen. The toes were barely visible sticking out through the end of two red balloons that looked ready to pop.

The phone. I rolled over to the other side of the bed and hung over the side, resting my hands on the floor. Blood from my nose spotted the carpet. I took down one knee, then the other, and crawled to the phone. It made me very happy to realize that I had remembered the number.

When I asked the lady for "Detective Stienert, please," my voice sounded funny. I felt for my nose and it wasn't there. There was some flesh there that felt like a sock full of mashed potatoes, but no nose.

Stienert picked up right away and it made me happy. "No nose, Moon."

"What?"

"No nose," I repeated.

"Moon? Little Moon?"

"Yeah. Yeah, it's me. Can you trace calls?"

"Uh-huh, it takes a while. You okay, Little Moon?"

"No, I'm all banged up. I think my legs are broken. My nose is broken and I don't know where I am. Trace the call, Moon. Bring an ambulance. Bring everybody. Bring the marines, bring the—"

Husky Voice took a breath.

"Gotta go."

I dropped the phone. I could hear Stienert yelling, "Moon, Little Moon." Husky Voice still had that transmitter and I lay down on my back and began working on the collar buckle. I tore a nail.

Husky Voice took a deeper breath.

The collar came off. I crawled on elbows and knees to get a clear look at him. He was turning over on his side, holding his head, facing away from me. He raised up on one arm and looked up onto the bed.

I said, "I got loose, Bruce," and he turned around.

"Lay back down, clown." I was on my stomach, holding the gun out in front of me with both hands.

He lay down on his back, turned to look at me again. "Damn."

We stayed like that for several minutes. He breathed in and out loudly and so did I, through my mouth. It was a duet.

There were sirens in the distance, beautiful melodic police sirens. Tires screeched and footsteps hit the porch running. "Here they come, chum."

Stienert came in first, Baker was right behind him. Stienert looked at me and I smiled at him and he looked away. Baker looked at me over Stienert's shoulder and said, "Jesus."

The pain came back. It was all over this time. Two guys came in with white coats and black bags. They knelt down beside me and looked me over, touching and feeling. One of them bent over me with a stethoscope and pressed it against my chest. He said, "Morphine." The other guy said, "Yeah."

Morphine is very good stuff.

▲ *17* ▲

MOM AND DAD were there the first time. She had a small handkerchief wadded up in her hand and was wiping the side of her nose. She looked down at me with her head tilted. Dad was standing behind her, his hands on her shoulders.

Someone was on the other side of the bed, the left side. I started to turn my head that way. The left eye wasn't working. I wrinkled my face. There were bandages on the nose and over the left eye. A nurse leaned over me. Her face was blurry, but the white cap gave her away. She said, "Hi."

I looked at her, trying to bring her into focus.

"You have a tracheal tube," she said. "It helps you to breathe, but it's also why you can't talk. Blink your eye if you can understand."

Blink your eye? Eye? Just one?

"If you can hear me, blink your eye."

Blink? I knew what blink meant. I thought about it, then blinked my eye slowly.

Dad's voice said, "Atta-boy."

Somebody held my hand. The nurse shone a bright light in my eye and said, "That's good." The light went away. The nurse's head came back into view. She said, "I'm going to give you another shot so you'll sleep some more."

It sounded good to me. I tried to smile, but there were some kinds of strings in my mouth. I felt the needle go in my left arm.

When I came to the second time I had legs and they were letting me know it. The room was dimly lit. Someone was patting my right hand. I wanted to look that way, but it was too much trouble. Whoever it was whispered, "Nurse."

Another white cap and blurry face. She said, "I hear you like Ray Charles."

I managed a nod.

"Me too. You want to talk?"

I said a silent "Yes." No sound came out.

The nurse-face said, "Take your time now. You can't talk because you have an airway. Just breathe. When I tell you to talk just say a few words. Then breathe some more."

I tried to say Okay, but nothing came out.

Something was pressing against my throat. I said, "Hello." Several people said "Hi."

I moved my head a little and saw fuzzy figures at the right of the bed. Someone was squeezing my hand and I squeezed back. It felt good to do that.

The light shone into my right eye, then moved toward the left. The nurse said, "Can you see the light, Chris?"

She pressed against my throat. I said, "Right eye. Left eye gone."

"It's not gone, Chris. Do you have a headache?"

Headache? My tongue was sore. I ran it around my mouth and felt a couple of chipped teeth.

"Does your head hurt?"

I thought about my head. "Some."

Someone on the right was crying. The nurse took my right hand and raised it to my neck. My fingers touched a tube. She said, "Feel that?"

I nodded.

"If you want to talk, just press here. Like this—put a finger over the hole."

She put my finger over the hole and my breath stopped. I pulled it away and could breath again. I took a deeper breath and put my finger back over the hole. "Who is here?"

Mom said, "I'm here, Chris. So is your father."

Vicki's voice said, "Hi, Chris," and Stienert said, "Hey, Moon."

Hands touched my arms and shoulders and face. Wonderful, gentle hands.

I dozed off again and woke up in the dark. My mouth was dry. I raised my hand to my face and felt around. The nose was bandaged, the left eye was covered, and there was some stitching in the lip. Someone moved in the dark. "You okay, Chris?"

"Leon?"

"Uh-huh. They said not to turn on the light."

I said, "Don't fart in here, Leon."

Leon clomped over to the bed. He must have been wearing his boots. I raised my hand and he took it. Leon had big hands. "Chris, you look awful."

"Feel awful," I said.

Leon patted my hand. "I ring for the nurse."

The nurse fussed around with the pillows and told me the doctor was on his way. She did the light-in-the-eye trick again, lifting some kind of patch when she did the left eye. It must have been important to her. A little light got through the left eye that time. I put my finger over the tube. "Eye better."

The doctor asked Leon to leave. He did the light-in-the-eye thing and said, "Good. Pretty good."

Someone turned up the lights. I was focusing pretty well now. The doctor was a curly-haired guy with brown eyes. "How you feel?"

I said, "Better."

"Tell me more."

I plugged the hole again. "Legs hurt, mouth dry." I took a breath. "Head hurts, neck hurts, back hurts." A breath. "My legs broken?"

He nodded. "Yes, avulsion fractures of both tibias. Not too serious. A concussion. Hematoma behind left eye that seems to be subsiding. Multiple contusions, plantar surface of both feet. Some stitches in your lip and your nose is busted all to hell."

I said, "Should see the other guy."

The doctor said, "I have. I want to let you stay awake for a while without sedation or painkillers. As the medication wears off you're going to start feeling more pain. Don't worry about it. We can always knock you out again if it gets too bad."

I nodded.

"The pain that you will be feeling is healing pain. You won't be getting worse. Things heal better, things heal quicker without a lot of dope in you, but don't let it get too bad. When it starts to get bad, let us know."

"Okay."

"Then we will have to put you under one more time and take out the airway. You want your nose back the way it was?"

"Yeah, I guess."

"We did the best we could," he said. "My name is Dr. Gewertz." I raised my hand and he shook it. "You want that kid back in here with you?"

I nodded and he turned to the nurse. "Crank him up."

The nurse cranked me up and left the room behind the doctor. Leon came back in. He said, "Everybody coming over to see you."

"What day is it, Leon."

Leon thought a moment. His glasses were crooked again. I motioned for him to come closer and straightened them. "I don't know. Chris. You been in here, you been here a whole day."

"Pull the sheet down, Leon."

"Huh?"

"Pull the sheet down," I took another breath. "I want look at legs."

Leon said, "Ah, don't do that, Chris."

"Let me see them."

Leon stood up and looked around. "The nurse be back in a minute."

"Pull down the sheet, Leon."

Leon pulled the sheet down slowly. When he got below my knees he made little whimpering sounds. They looked like blue elephant legs. The skin was shiny and tight and the pores looked like nail holes.

Leon was crying softly. "I kill that man, Chris. he ever get out of jail, I kill that man."

Stienert came in, carrying some flowers. He walked over to the bed and held them up. "These from Baker, Moon." He put the flowers on a little metal table. "How you feel?"

"Fair." I was getting better at working with the airway. "Look at my legs, will you, Moon?"

"I saw them before."

"What do you think?"

He sat on the left of the bed and looked at my face. "You sure ugly."

Mom and Dad came in with Willa, Sampson, and Billy. They all gathered around the bed and looked at me. Stienert said, "He not as bad as he looks. Everybody look like this they get beat up, get they nose broke."

Mom said, "You look fine, Chris."

Dad said, "No, he doesn't, Rachel. He looks terrible, but that's normal."

Mom cried into her handkerchief. "Don't tell him that. He needs encouragement."

"But he's got to know."

Mom said, "He used to have such a pretty face."

Dad said, "Come here." They moved back into a corner of the room and argued softly. Same old routine.

Vicki came in with a man she introduced as her father and everybody stood around and stared at me. They were probably trying to think of something to say. So was I. Mom and Dad continued a whispered argument in the corner of the room.

Vicki's dad said, "It's raining out. Nice soaking rain."

Sampson said, "We been needing rain."

Billy said, "That guy was a professional, Chris. A professional killer."

"He used to have such a pretty face," Mom said from the corner.

A wave of pain came up from my legs. If they were healing pains, the legs were healing at top speed. I tried to wiggle the toes and couldn't tell if anything was happening or not.

I asked Stienert, "How is he, the guy that beat me up?"

"Skull fracture."

"Why did he talk like that?"

"Somebody slit his throat a few years ago. He's a bad dude. About twenty arrests, no convictions. Witnesses all dead."

"He did it real cold, Moon." I breathed in. "He wasn't mad at me or anything. It was like he was just doing a job, taking care of business."

Dr. Gewertz came into the room and stood by the bed. "How's it going?"

"Legs are hurting more."

"How about the feet—do they hurt?"

I concentrated. "No, sir. It's from the ankles to the knees."

"Okay." He turned around. "Will you folks step out into the hall for a minute?"

I said, "Could Moon stay?"

Dr. Gewertz said, "Yes, he can stay."

They shuffled out of the room. I should have asked if my father could stay instead of Stienert. It probably made him feel bad and he would take it out on Mom.

Dr. Gewertz pulled up the sheet. "The kind of fractures you have are like cracks and chips in a plate. The edges are still together and they should heal satisfactorily in time. Neither of your leg bones is cracked all the way through." He pressed the top of my shins. "Your legs are blue from all the internal bleeding. We've got to worry about blood clots later on."

I started worrying about them right away, imagining little

scabs floating around in my vessels looking for a place to lodge.

He picked up a little pizza cutter from a tray and held it up. "Called a pinwheel." He rolled it along my arm. It felt like a track of pin pricks, not quite painful enough to ouch about. "Close your eyes."

He ran the pinwheel along the outside of my right leg "Feel that?"

"Uh-huh. Right leg."

He did the inside of the right leg, then both sides of the left leg, and I felt everything.

"Feel this?"

"No, sir."

"How about this?"

"No."

"This?"

"No."

"How about here?"

"A little bit. Top of foot. Right foot."

"Very good. Open your eyes." He did the light in the eyes. I noticed more light in the left eye this time and he saw something that made him happy.

He sat down on the edge of the bed. "I saw the tape," he said. He pressed his lips together. "Your friend here thought I should see it and he brought the cassette over. Terrible. Saw the whole thing. When you were hitting him on the head, when you came around and hit him . . . I was rooting for you. Shouted 'Hit him again, hit him again.' "

He stood and walked over to look out the window. "They've scheduled him for surgery. Not a major operation. Drill a small hole in his skull. He just needs a drain for intercranial hemorrhage. I was supposed to do it but had to pull out. First time I ever declined surgery. I couldn't trust myself."

Stienert said, "Let me do it. I drill him."

Dr. Gewertz smiled. "That's the way I felt."

I plugged my tube. "How about feet?"

"Yes, your feet. Listen up, I'll tell you what I know, what I don't know. There are some maybes too."

"Okay."

"Your eye is getting better and should be all right. Your nose might look funny. That's a maybe. The legs, along in here"—he rubbed the tops of my shins—"they should heal up okay. Some knots in them, but they should be okay. The feet have nerve damage. Lots of maybes with the feet."

"What's the worst maybe?"

"The worst?" he said. "The worst is that your feet will always be numb, the ankles weak. You'd have to wear some sort of prosthetic high-top boots. Be subject to ankle sprains. Maybe develop some arthritis. Never walk normally."

"What's the best?"

Dr. Gewertz said, "You could be good as ever."

"What's the odds?"

He shrugged. "Fifty-fifty."

Stienert said, "Moon'll make it."

Dr. Gewertz said, "I'm going to stay on duty. Take the pain as long as you can, then we'll put you under and take out your airway. You can eat then."

The doctor left and everybody came back into the room. Stienert told them what the doctor had said and did it just right. He moved the odds to ninety-ten, my favor.

We ran out of things to say after a while and the pain was heating up some. I acted like I was getting sleepy so that they could go without feeling guilty. I asked Dad to crank down the bed for me. "I think I can sleep now."

Mom said, "Sleep is what you need."

They said their good-byes and filed out of the room. I lay there in the half light, trying to will some feeling into my feet. I imagined feeling coursing down my back, my legs, feet, and toes.

The nurse came in. She was very pretty, auburn hair, brown eyes, a trim figure, maybe twenty-five or twenty-six.

She smiled at me. "Everything okay?"

"Yes, thanks."

"Would you like the TV on?"

"No." Some pain came up from the legs. Bad pain, and I panicked for a moment. Healing pains, he had said. Was that the truth or bedside-manner jargon?

The nurse opened the blinds. Rivulets of rain patterned the window. As drops slid down the glass they joined with other drops to form the rivulets. She came back over to the bed and took my pulse at the wrist. "Anything I can do for you?"

"Talk," I said.

"What you want to talk about?"

"Anything. Not the weather."

She pushed away the TV. "Well, you're a big star on TV, on the news. There are reporters out in the waiting room, waiting to get at you. Dr. Gewertz won't let them in. They'll be waiting for me with their questions when I go off duty. Anything you want me to tell them?"

"TV sucks," I said.

She laughed. "I'll tell them. Anything else?"

I said, "Could I be alone awhile?"

"Sure. I'll take a break." She put something in my hand. "You press this if you need anything."

When Billy and I were building the shack, five years ago, Billy had smacked his thumb with a hammer. You could tell it really hurt. He sat next to Mote and watched me work, holding his left thumb with his right hand down between his legs, with his shoulders hunched. He rocked back and forth and said, "What kind of roof are we going to put on?"

Mote said, "Hurts bad, doesn't it?"

Billy shook his head. "Not too bad."

"As long as you try to run from the pain, it will keep chasing after you. Go ahead and experience the pain, Billy."

Billy dropped his head and rocked some more.

"Feel it. Let it be as bad as it can be."

Billy said, "Why?"

"Just do it. Think about how bad it hurts."

Billy crossed his arms on his chest, protecting his swollen thumb.

"Terrible, isn't it?"

Billy nodded. Some tears ran down his cheeks. "Yes."

"You're crying because it hurts like hell, aren't you?"

Billy looked at him.

I said, "Hey. Cut it out, Mote."

Mote ignored me. "Worst pain you ever had?"

Billy nodded. "Yeah."

Mote said, "Probably the most pain anyone has ever had. Think you are going to die from it?"

Billy said, "No." He was still rocking, but he smiled a little bit.

"Just spend the rest of your life holding your thumb, crying?"

Billy laughed and snuffled his nose.

Mote said, "Hey, quit the laughing or I won't feel sorry for you anymore. Besides, you laugh at pain and it loses its grip on you. You don't want that to happen, do you?"

Billy leaned over and bumped his shoulder against Mote's. Then he stood up and got his hammer and went back to work. When he sobbed an involuntary racking breath, Mote said, "Crybaby," and Billy laughed really hard.

I let the pain come—the legs, back, head screamed with it. Total pain. I thought, *This is a mistake,* but made myself immerse myself in the hurt. The pain engulfed me as I swam around in it. It was red. Red with yellow edges. I had the call button in my right hand. If I pressed the button, the nurse would give me something for the pain.

I felt sorry for myself. Why me? I watched myself feeling sorry for myself. Poor Chris, I thought. I thought about how my face must look, contorted with pain and self-pity. Suddenly I was a spectator to the whole mess. It was there, the pain was there, but I was partly detached from it, above the pain.

The hell with the pain. Pain meant that I was alive. Lot

better than being dead. If I hadn't hit Husky Voice, I would probably be dead now.

Dr. Gewertz came back in and stood over me. "How's it going?"

I took a breath and pressed the tube again. "Like to get this thing out. Eat."

"Let's do it." He pulled out a syringe and squirted a drop at the ceiling. I felt the sting in the arm. It was powerful stuff. "Sleep tight, Chris."

He left the room and I felt myself sinking.

The door opened. Willa walked to the bed and leaned over to kiss my cheek. I was going to black, even with my eyes open. "I'm sorry," she said. "My fall. Saw my fall."

▲ *18* ▲

RASPING BREATH, in and out. He was back. I kept my eyes closed and tried to locate the sound, searching the room with my hearing. In the room, right in the room, and very close.

I stopped breathing so that I could listen better and the rasping stopped. When I breathed again the rasping started back up. I smiled at myself, relieved. Scared of my own breathing. It reminded me of something, something I had read somewhere, but I couldn't remember what it was.

Sunlight was slanting in a side window, either sunrise or sunset. I raised a hand to my throat. The tube was gone. The bandages were off my left eye. I palmed my right eye. I had dim vision in my left now.

The pretty nurse was looking down at me. "How you doing?"

"Okay," I said. "Water?"

"Sure." She brought over a glass with a bent straw in it and helped prop me up with pillows. Her smile was a dazzler.

I took a sip of water, then another, and let it wash around in my mouth. I decided that I would drink water for about two hours. The nurse tugged at the glass and I tugged back. "Easy," she said. "Not too much."

I remembered what it was that I had read. *"Robinson Crusoe,"* I said.

"What?"

"Robinson Crusoe, scared of his own footprints."

"You okay, honey?"

"Water."

I drank about half the glass. All the cells of my body were having a good time. I could feel them sucking up the water.

"You want some breakfast?"

"Yes." I tried to read her badge. "What's your name?"

"Ms. Anderson," she said. She cranked me into a sitting position and pushed a cart against the bed. The top swung out over my lap. There was a bowl of some kind of gruel, a glass of orange juice, and some red Jell-O. I looked over to the right. Stienert was lying on the other bed, asleep.

My cells gave me another round of applause for the orange juice and a standing ovation when I swallowed the gruel stuff. Wonderful food, but I filled up after half a bowl.

Ms. Anderson sat by the bed and watched me eat. When I pushed the food away she said, "You'll do better next time." She nodded at Stienert. "Do you want me to wake him?"

"No, let him sleep."

Stienert opened an eye. "I'm awake, Moon." He sat up and rubbed his eyes. He had slept in his clothes. His shirt was wrinkled and his tie was loosened. "How you feel?"

"Better."

Stienert stood up and stretched, with his hands in the small of his back. Ms. Anderson left the room. He pulled over a chair and turned the back toward me, sitting down with his forearms on the backrest. He put his chin on his wrist. "Funny case."

"What's going on?"

"Somebody tossed your house last night, searching for that book, I guess. They searched your friend's house too."

"What's in the book, do you know?"

He shook his head. "No idea."

"How about the guy that beat me up?"

"Bulloch a heavyweight. High-priced hit man, free-lance." He scratched his head. "Case won't connect up. Can't get a handle on it."

"Who was Bulloch working for?"

"Don't know. He won't talk. Been busted lots of times and knows the ropes. He's been connected to the black mafia a few times, nothing you could prove."

"Black mafia?"

"Uh-huh."

"I never heard of a black mafia."

Nurse Anderson came back with a cup of coffee and handed it to Stienert. He said, "Thank you, ma'am," and took a noisy sip. "Black mafia not real organized. Not like the other guys, the real Mafia."

I said, "Is Bulloch a black guy?"

"Yeah. Didn't you know?"

"No. He had on that mask. He had on rubber gloves."

Stienert drank the rest of his coffee and laid down his cup. "I watched the tape. What happened? How you get to the house?"

I told him the whole story. Ms. Anderson listened for a while, then picked up Stienert's cup. "Want some more?"

Stienert nodded.

I said, "How about the guy in the VW?"

He shook his head. "Dead end. Finally traced the guy. Turned out he was in California when Holder was killed."

"Who was it?"

"Just some guy."

"What guy?"

"Nobody you know."

"What was his name?"

"None of your business."

Ms. Anderson came in with another coffee for Stienert. He said, "I think Holder the kind of guy most women would cheat on."

"Why?"

"I don't know. He strike you as loving, caring, gentle?"

I thought a moment. "No, I guess not."

Stienert finished his coffee and went into the bathroom. Ms. Anderson said, "Do you want any more breakfast?"

"I'd like some more orange juice."

"I'll get you some. When I get back tell your friend good-bye. Have to give you a bath."

"A bath?"

"Uh-huh."

"Where?"

"In the bed. Just a sponge bath."

I said, "Ahh."

"What?"

I shook my head. "Nothing."

When Stienert came back I said, "She's going to give me a bath, Moon."

He smiled. "All right." He singsonged the words.

"Don't go. Tell her you have to stay, ask me some more questions or something."

"What you 'fraid of? She a nurse, do this all the time."

"I'm not afraid, it's just . . . you know."

Nurse Anderson came back, pushing a cart. She handed me a glass of juice and sat down in a chair with her arms crossed. The juice was wonderful. I said, "I know, Moon. I got an idea. Suppose you tell Bulloch that you know where the book is. Tell him you'll sell it. Then see who shows up."

He shook his head. "Can't do that. Called *entrapment*."

"You'll have to leave now," Ms. Anderson said.

Stienert said, "Okay."

I said, "Wait, Moon. Uh, how is Kate?"

"She fine. She come and see you soon." He started for the door. "See you later."

"Well, look," I said. "Where is Bulloch?"

Stienert pointed his thumb at the ceiling. "Fifth floor."

"Well, shouldn't you stay? What if he comes for me?"

"There's a cop on his door, Moon. You don't have to worry about him." He opened the door. "You got to worry about her."

Ms. Anderson was smiling at me. She cranked me down and wheeled over the cart. She pulled the sheet up from the bottom to expose my legs.

"Maybe I could walk," I said. "Maybe I could walk to the shower."

"No walking," she said. "Not for a while." She was washing my feet. I still didn't have any feeling in them, but I could tell she was washing them. The water felt good on my legs. She was gentle and careful and as she bent over I could look down her blouse. She raised her eyes quickly and caught me looking.

A little message came up from my penis. I tried to ignore it, but it made a little tent with the sheet. When Ms. Anderson turned to wring out her cloth, I pushed it down. She finished the top and sides of my legs and said, "Turn on your side."

It took a while and when I got on my side I kept my leg in an uncomfortable position and tried to concentrate on the pain. It was working and the tent disappeared.

She did the back of my legs and then washed my back and shoulders. "Doing okay?"

"Yes, ma'am."

She started cleaning my behind. I was saying to myself, Please don't get a hard-on, please don't get a hard-on.

My penis said, Hey, Chris. This pretty lady is going to turn us over soon.

"Turn over."

My penis said, Oh, boy! and came to life. I bit my bottom lip, hard.

"Turn over on your back."

My penis said, Wait till she sees this.

Ms. Anderson put a hand on my shoulder and pressed backward. "Turn over now. I need to wash your front."

I said, "I think I can take over from here. I mean, I think I can reach the rest of it."

"Turn over."

I turned over. Please don't be hard, please don't be hard. Please don't be . . .

"My, my," she said. "Like a little soldier." I had my eyes shut, but I heard her walk away into the bathroom. "I'm going to change the water," she said from the sink. "Give you a minute to calm down."

I laid there and thought about snakes. I imagined being in a room full of big snakes, all of them looking at me, coiled and ready to strike, flicking their nasty tongues in and out.

She began washing my chest. I had my eyes shut. I could feel the little soldier jumping and throbbing. It said, How 'bout me? How 'bout me?

She washed my face very gently. I opened an eye, just a slit, and she was looking at me. I shut the eye again. "I'm sorry."

She said, "Don't apologize."

The soldier was doing Present Arms. Ms. Anderson bathed my stomach with slow, circular motions. I tried to think of something to say, but nothing seemed appropriate. I could have asked her about the weather, but she would probably have guessed that I had other things on my mind.

I put my hands over my eyes, which made a lot of sense. "This is really terrible. I'm sorry."

"Quit saying you're sorry, honey. I've seen erections before, hundreds of them. Don't worry about it." She dried off my chest and stomach.

Hundreds? I wanted to ask her how mine compared with the others. Average? Superior? Below average?

Ms. Anderson said, "Here" and handed me a washrag. "Clean that little rascal."

She turned away and crossed her arms. I got busy cleaning myself. It seemed to calm the soldier a bit, about halfway, down to a semi. She handed me a towel without turning around and I dried off and pulled the sheet back up. "I'm done."

"You men," she said. "You men are so silly about your erections."

"I'm sorry."

"No, don't say you're sorry." She laughed again. "That's what I mean. You men are sorry when you have one and miserable when you can't. So ashamed when you get caught with one at the wrong time, so proud when you get one at the right time."

"I'm not proud of this one," I said.

"I know. I know you couldn't help it. I guess it was almost a kind of compliment." She took a basin of water into the bathroom and poured it out. "I guess women are funny too, come to think of it. If there ever comes a time that I don't cause that to happen, I'll probably feel bad."

She wheeled the cart to the door. "Some people to see you," she said. "Some reporters and TV people. Are you ready?"

"Hey, you know what?"

She shook her head. "What?"

"My feet. I think I've got a little feeling in my feet now."

She laughed. "Probably moved the swelling around."

A WOMAN CAME into the room carrying an attaché case and a clipboard. She was followed by two men with camera equipment and a man I recognized from the eleven-o'clock news. He had a square jaw, wavy blond hair, blue eyes, and lots of teeth. The woman walked briskly to the window and opened the blinds. Dr. Gewertz came in and sat in a chair with a cup of coffee.

The cameramen talked back and forth to each other. The woman with the clipboard went over to the newsman and had him read some papers. He nodded and turned to the mirror. The lady came to the bed and stared at my face. Then she put the attaché case down on the bed and opened it. She looked at my face again.

I said, "Hi."

She mumbled, "Hello," pulled something out of the case, and reached for my face.

I said, "What are you doing?"

"Just a little makeup," she said. "Don't be nervous."

"I don't want any makeup."

"It won't hurt," she said. "I just want to highlight these bruises a bit." She leaned back and her hand hit my leg. I yelped.

"Oh, that's right," she said. "Your legs are broken, aren't they?" She stood up and snatched the sheet up from my feet and legs. "John, let's get a close-up of these legs."

John looked at my legs and kind of winced. He glanced up at me and our eyes met. He said, "Sorry, kid." Then he leaned over and took close-ups of my feet and legs.

The lady came around to the side of the bed. "Just hold still—this won't take a minute."

It took about three minutes. She leaned back and admired her work. "Okay, Rick. We're ready for you."

Rick took one more look in the mirror and came over to the bed. The lady gave him a microphone and adjusted the lapels of his jacket. He read from the clipboard, then handed it back to her and faced the cameras.

The lady backed away and said, "Start cameras. It's all yours, Rick."

Rick said, "Good evening. This is Rick Cantrell, *Channel 9 Action News,* on location at City Hospital. I'm here with young Chris Miller who, two nights ago, was the victim of a savage beating. Later in this broadcast you'll see actual films of the beating."

John and his camera were at the foot of the bed. The other one was at the side aimed at my face.

Rick said, "Tell me, Chris, how are you feeling?"

I said, "Your hair sure is pretty."

Rick didn't quite know what to do. The lady yelled, "Cut!" John was having trouble hiding his laughter and Dr. Gewertz must have swallowed his coffee wrong. He was bent over, coughing.

Rick said, "I thought this was all set up."

"It was," the lady said. "It was supposed to be." She came around to stand by Rick and look down at me. "Is there some problem, Mr. Miller?"

"Yeah. I don't like you people," I said. "Except him." I pointed to the laughing cameraman, John. Rick and the lady looked at him and he shrugged.

"Well, like us or not, we are here to get a news story and you might as well cooperate."

I didn't say anything.

The lady turned on her heel and walked to the door,

slapping the clipboard against her thigh. She went out and I lay there and sulked. Rick went back to the mirror and checked his hair. The lady came back in with my father.

Dad said, "What's the trouble, Chris?"

"I don't want to do this, Dad. It's embarrassing and these people are scary."

"Well, look, they're just doing their job."

"So was the guy that beat me up."

"Go ahead and let them get on with it." He came closer to the bed. "They promised to mention my company. You know, let you give me a plug. It would be great for business."

"Aw, come on, Dad. Don't ask me to do that."

Dad sat on the bed and held my hands. The lady said, "Get a shot of that."

Dad whispered, "I made a deal with them, Chris. They get to interview you and show the tapes of you getting beat up."

"What kind of deal? What do you get?"

"They mention my company and pick up the hospital bill. Our insurance doesn't cover all of this."

"You should have asked me, Dad."

He shook his head. "You're still under eighteen. I'm trying to do what's best for you."

"Did you sign something?"

"Yeah, I signed a consent form."

"Aw, nuts." I looked at the woman and nodded my head.

They all got back in their original positions. Rick sat on the bed and went through his introduction all over again. He said, "How are you feeling, Chris?"

I said, "Pretty bad, Rick. I feel better now, though, now that you're here. You're my favorite newsperson."

"Thank you." He smiled and glanced up at the camera. "I understand that the beating had something to do with racism. What are your feelings about racism, Chris?"

"I don't have any."

"None at all?" Rick sounded shocked. "No feelings at all?"

"Well, yeah, I guess I'm against it, but . . . Well, the idea that blacks are all bad and whites are all good is such a silly

idea that I never thought about it very much. It's like if you
tell me that the earth is flat. I would just figure that you're a
dumb guy. I wouldn't have any real strong feelings about it."

Rick said, "So, in your opinion, racism is a bankrupt
philosophy?"

"Uh-huh. I wish everybody would get off that. Get off
racism and get on with things that matter. My father owns
Miller Engineering," I said. "At Miller Engineering we have
draftsmen, engineers, land planners, and machinists of all
races and creeds, working together in harmony."

"I see."

"Over fifteen years of technical excellence."

"I understand," Rick said. He had a deep baritone voice.
"Tell me, Chris. What thoughts crossed your mind as you
were being tortured and beaten?"

"Pain," I said. "How much it hurt. Fear. About what
you'd expect, I guess. I mean, I wasn't thinking about ending
world hunger or peace in the Middle East or saving the
whales."

Rick nodded.

"I keep up with all the world events on *Channel 9 Action
News*. I always watch *Channel 9 Action News* before going to
bed. My favorite part is the way you joke around with the
weatherman."

Rick said, "Thank you."

I said, "There is some kind of book involved in all this. A
green ledger and if anybody knows about it, I would sure
like to have it. The police would like to have it."

Rick said, "But despite the pain and despite the fear and
broken bones, you managed to overcome and subdue your
attacker." He was reading from the clipboard the lady held
up out of camera range. "How did one so young react with
such courage?"

"I don't know. I was just scared and I didn't want him to
beat me anymore." I started to think about the beating. It
made my legs hurt and I shivered under the sheets.

"It must have been a terrible ordeal," Rick said.

I started to cry like a little baby.

From the corner of the room Dr. Gewertz said, "That's enough."

The lady nodded. "Just a few more seconds." She told the cameraman, "Get a close-up of his face."

John said, "No." He pointed his camera at Rick and so did the other guy.

Rick said, "I'm sure that the prayers of our viewers are for your rapid recovery. This is Rick Cantell, *Channel 9 Action News.*"

While they interviewed Dr. Gewertz, Dad came over to the bed and held my hand. He didn't say he was sorry, but I think he was.

The TV people left and Dr. Gewertz went through his examination again. There was more feeling in the feet. He removed the bandages from my face and pressed around on my nose. "You're improving very quickly," he said.

He went to the dresser and came back with a hand mirror. I looked at my face. It was fascinating—black, blue, red, swollen, and puffy. I said, "How much of this is permanent?"

"Probably none," he said. "You'll probably look about the same as you used to."

"I was hoping for better. How long do I stay here?"

"I want that swelling down more in the legs. Three days, maybe four. You're going to be in a wheelchair for a while after you leave. Probably another few weeks. After visiting hours we'll start you on physical therapy."

Mom, Dad, the Walkers, Billy, his mom, Vicki, and Mr. Sherman all came in together. There were so many people in the room that there was no one to talk to. "They treating you okay?" "Anything you need?" "You look well," "Be up in no time," "They feeding you good?" "Isn't this a nice room?" "Comfortable?" and like that.

Billy said, "Our house is a mess. So is yours."

"Yeah. Moon told me. Sorry."

Billy's mom said, "Don't you worry." She patted my hand. "It's spring-cleaning time anyway."

Vicki was looking at me. I wondered if there was any way that she could know about what had happened with Ms. Anderson.

There was a long pause. I said, "Everybody leave their phone number. I'll call you later on, one at a time. It will be easier to talk and you don't have to come here, miss work."

Vicki said, "Call me at your house. Willa and I are going over to help your mother clean up."

Billy said, "Stienert and Baker are here. They want to talk to us together."

There was another long silence before Dad said, "Mom and I have to go, Chris. We'll talk to you later." Everybody lined up for handshakes and kisses. Vicki gave me a wonderful mouth kiss. Our first. Mr. Sherman shook my hand and told me that the University of Georgia was interested in giving me a scholarship if I recovered. Then they all filed out.

Stienert and Baker came in and pulled up chairs around the bed. Baker had his hairpiece on again. He said, "We want to go over this whole case with you guys. See if we can come up with something."

Stienert said, "Everybody tell all they know. Maybe something will tie together."

I said, "Do you think whoever killed Holder was after the ledger?"

Baker shook his head. "Why didn't he take it when he did the killing?"

I hadn't thought of that before. It was a good question.

"Here's what we know," Stienert said. "Somebody killed Holder about ten o'clock. Evidence all points to Thomas, your pal Mote. Murder weapon, motive, opportunity."

I said, "Mote told me he had waded the creek that morning, down to that big hole of water. It's a long walk, several hours each way. So if you'll just believe his story for a minute, somebody could have gone to the shack and gotten a knife and killed Holder between nine and ten."

Billy said, "It could have been the guy in the Volkswagen that was, you know, the guy who was seeing Mrs. Holder."

"Nope. We tracked him down. He was out of town last Thursday. Could have been the guy who wanted the ledger," Stienert said. "Maybe he saw Mrs. Holder coming, and split."

I said, "How about Bulloch? You get anything out of him?"

Baker shook his head. "Nope. We might. We have him charged with kidnapping, attempted murder. Maybe if we offer to reduce it to assault, he'll give us something."

Stienert said, "Is there anything you kids holding back? Anything you haven't told us?"

I said, "How about ERWA? What about those guys?"

Stienert said, "More than we thought. They bigger than we thought. Started four years ago, but they didn't start small."

"How do you mean, Moon?"

"Sprung up all at once in nine cities. Now they in twenty-four. Usually that kind of thing starts small and grows slow."

Billy said, "They must have some central leadership."

Baker said, "Yeah."

A very big young man came in wearing a white orderly outfit, pushing a wheelchair. He had long, curly blond hair tied in a ponytail and wore sunglasses. There was an earring in one ear. "I'm supposed to take you to therapy now."

Stienert asked if he could help lift me and the orderly smiled and said, "No." He came around to the bed and put his hands under my knees and shoulders. He had a badge that said David. He lifted me into the wheelchair like I was his child, then strapped me in and tucked a sheet around me.

We all got on the elevator together. David pushed Six and we rode up and got off. Stienert pushed One and waved good-bye.

David said, "John Wayne was my idol." He was pushing me down a long corridor.

"Oh, yeah? Did you see him on TV the other day, some kind of war movie?"

"Yep," he said in a John Wayne voice. *The Sands of Imer Jeemer*. That's my favorite."

I said, "My favorite is *True Grit*."

"That was good," David agreed. "There's a John Wayne movie on tonight."

"Is it a good one?"

He pushed me through double swinging doors. "There ain't no such thing as a bad John Wayne movie." David went through some papers on a desk. "You get the whirlpool."

He pushed me down a hall and we went into a room with a whirlpool in the center. There was an old guy in the whirlpool already and an orderly sitting on a bench, reading *Guns and Ammo* magazine. David took off his shoes and trousers and my sheet, then pushed me down a ramp into the whirlpool, wheelchair and all. It was hot and the jets were strong enough to hurt my legs a little.

David said, "Are you okay?"

I said, "Doing just fine, Pilgrim" in my John Wayne voice. I do a pretty good John Wayne.

David liked it a lot. "Say something else."

I said, "Don't try it, Liberty."

David was easily amused. "That's really good," he said. "You're going to have to teach me that."

▲ 20 ▲

I SLEPT FOR several hours after the whirlpool and woke up hungry. When I rang the buzzer a different nurse came in. My eyes were getting better and I could read her nametag: Doreen. She fussed around with me for a while and cranked me up into a sitting position. "They've been showing you on TV," she said. "You're a star."

I thought about the way my face looked. "Maybe I'll get a movie contract," I said. "One of those monster movies."

Doreen left me and returned with a tray of food and a big stack of mail and packages. I ate and went through the mail, mostly get-well cards from kids at school. I saved the packages for last.

One package had no return address. I forced the string over the corner and removed the paper. It was a green ledger. The green ledger! I opened it up and looked at the first page. It was hand-printed gibberish. At first I thought it was a foreign language, until I noticed some of the words had numbers in them. It was some kind of code.

I looked back inside the wrapping and found a note. It said:

> Saw you on television. We was looking for copies of exams and took this by mistake and didn't mean to get you in trouble.

I rang the buzzer and when Doreen came asked her to bring me some paper and a pencil so that I could write some letters. A master of deception. When she brought the paper I copied all the handprinted pages. It took about a half hour and by the time I was finished, I had a plan. I called Detective Stienert.

When he answered I said, "Moon, how hard would it be to put a tap on Bulloch's phone?"

"What for?"

"Could you do it?"

"Kind of hard. Lot of red tape. Why you want a tap?"

"I can't explain it now, but if you can get a tap he will be calling out . . . He will call the people who hired him in about three or four hours."

"How you know?"

"Just do it, Moon. Trust me."

He was silent, thinking. "Probably do it through the switchboard. Wouldn't have to go into his room."

"Do it, Moon."

"I'll try. I'll talk to Baker."

"Three hours, Moon. He'll be calling out about then."

"You sure?"

"Yes."

"Okay. I see what I can do."

I rang the buzzer again. It was a few minutes before Doreen came in. I asked her if she could get in touch with David, the orderly who took me up to therapy. She said she would.

David came sauntering in with a toothpick in his mouth. I said, "You know, you do walk like the Duke."

He grinned. "Yeah."

"David, I've got to ask you for a favor. You do me this favor and I'll teach you to talk like the Duke."

"What do you want?"

I handed him the ledger. "Can you hide this for me? Someplace that's safe but where you could get it in a hurry."

David took the book. "What's the story on you anyway?"

"What do you mean?"

"You're on TV. In the papers. Cops come to visit you. Are you some kind of agent or something?"

I said, "CIA." It just came out of my mouth.

David dropped the toothpick from his lips.

"Can I trust you, David?"

He shifted his weight. "Sure."

"I'm going to tell you some things that are top secret. It's a matter of national security. You can't tell anyone."

"Okay."

"That ledger contains secret coded messages that I captured from a Russian spy."

David looked through the pages of gibberish and said, "Wow!"

"It must not fall into enemy hands. I want you to keep it for me until we go to therapy at three."

"Real Commonest spies?"

"Yes, David. Russian spies who want to take over this country, do away with our beloved institutions, enslave our citizenry, and outlaw patriotic John Wayne movies."

"I'll do it," David said. He took the ledger.

"We'll need it after three, David. I am going to have another assignment for you then. But it must be secret—don't breathe a word."

"You can count on me," he said.

"Okay. Go hide the book. I have to work on this code."

David looked at the coded pages. "Wow!" he said. He put the book under his shirt and left.

The first page read:

H4. T394T3 HQT08
KBKV OQ4596 E4.
S86S866Q58, 9Y89 ZXMJN
(XJL) VKV XNKL

KM R4QTH365Q5896 T436QE3W. C 7P8 Q759HQ58SW,
JMMM 4976EW

9R QHH7685896, JK F492686T Q759HQ58S 48R03W,
JXMM 4976EW
QHH7685897.
Y8EE36 86 5476D 9R OQ458Q00A 43W5943E SQ4 86
TQ4QT3.

I looked at it for a long time and the letters started to blur
and run together. I rubbed my eyes. If the code was simple
enough for Holder to use, I was smart enough to figure it out.

The first four lines must have been a name, address, city,
and phone number. H4. could be Mr., Dr., or Ms. I decided
to try Mr. and began replacing the H's with M's and 4's with
R's.

Mr. ——R—— M——
——/—4.

The —4. must be the abbreviation for *Drive*, which meant
that the E's were D's. I put in a D.

The city had to be the S86S866Q58. The state would be
9Y89 Utah? Ohio? Iowa? The name of the city had ten
letters and the first three letters repeated. I scanned my brain
for repeated three-letter combinations. I got "Pompom" and
"Poopoo" and "Bambam" and "Dumdum" and "Doodoo." I
even came up with "Boiseboise," "Wallawalla," and thought
for a second that I had it with "Chachago, Illi." Brilliant.

I decided to do it alphabetically, starting with A. I tried
"Angang" and "Ackack" and went to B. "Booboo," "Bow-
wow." I took a deep breath and closed my eyes.

I thought I had something with "Cancan." "Caccanville,
Utah." Then there it was—my onboard computer came up
with it: Cincinnati. Ohio. Bingo! I started over with all the
letters from MR and DR and CINCINNATI, OHIO. It looked
like this:

Mr. ——OR——A——
——A——TON DR.

CINCINNATI, OHIO——
(XJL) VRV XNKL

—— —RA—M—NTATION ——NAD——, — ——I
A—TOMATI——, ——RO—ND— O— AMM—NI-
TION, —— —RO—NIN— A—TOMATI— RI————,
——— RO—ND— AMM—NI—ION.
HIDD—N IN TR—N—O——ARTIA——R——TOR—
D—AR IN —ARA——.

It was a start. I substituted F's for the three R's. The
two incomplete words became FRA—M— NTATION and
RIF——. The RIF—— had to be either RIFLES or RI-
FLED. I already had the D, so I used RIFLES and started to
make substitutions. MR. —EOR—E MA——, and stopped.
The —EOR—E had to be GEORGE. I started again and
got:

MR. GEORGE MAGL—
—— —A—TON DR.
CINCINNATI, OHIO ——
(XJL) VRV XNKL

—— FRAGMENTATION GRENADES, — ——I A—TO-
MATICS, ——— RO—UNDS OF AMM—NITION, ——
—RO—NING A—TOMATIC RIFLES, ——— RO—NDS
AMM—NITION.
—IDDEN IN TR—N— OF —ARTI——— RE—TORED
CAR IN GARAGE.

Jesus Christ! What the hell had Holder been up to? I filled
in some obvious letters and had:

Mr. George Magl—
—— Pa—ton Dr.
Cincinnati, Ohio——
(XJL) VRV XNKL

——Fragmentation grenades. — Uzi Automatics,———
rounds of ammunition, —— Browning automatic rifles,
————— rounds ammunition.

Hidden in trunk of partially restored car in garage.

I was starting on page two when the door opened and
David came in. It had taken two and a half hours to break
the code, but it seemed like ten minutes. He said, "I'm
ready."

"What's your last name, David?"

"Standridge."

"Raise your right hand and repeat after me."

David raised his hand.

I said, "I, David Standridge . . ."

"I, David Standridge," he said. He was standing at attention.

"Do hereby swear to uphold the Constitution of the United
States of America."

"Do hereby swear to hold up the Constitution of the
United States of America."

"And to the republic for which it stands."

"And to the republic for which it stands."

"And to oppose its enemies, both foreign and domestic."

" 'Pose its enemies, both foreign and domestic."

"And to support my local police."

"Support my local police."

"So help me God."

"So help me God."

We shook hands solemnly. "David, your code name is
Duke for this operation." David smiled and stood at ease.

"Did you hide the book somewhere where we can get at it
quickly?"

"Yes, sir."

"Duke, I want you to find out what room Mr. Bulloch is
in. He's on the next floor."

"Yes, sir."

David left the room and I dialed police headquarters. When
Stienert picked up I asked him if he got the phone tap set up.

"Nope. We tried, they turned us down, Moon."

I said, "Moon, some really heavy stuff is coming down. This ERWA outfit—they're involved in weapons or something."

"How you know?"

"I just know, that's all. I can force Bulloch's hand, get him to call his employers. You can bust up ERWA before they do something crazy, something violent."

Stienert was humming to himself.

I waited.

He said, "This don't work out, I'm out of a job."

"Are you going to do it?"

"Uh-huh. Give me a half hour. I'm going to do it on my own, no authorization. Illegal as hell."

David took me up to therapy and lowered me into the whirlpool. There was another guy in the pool with some kind of palsy problem. He sat on the ledge of the pool with his head down. His right hand made masturbation motions in his lap and I tried to ignore it. I hoped I never got that way. I wondered if it had anything to do with doing it too much.

After a half hour David pulled me out of the whirlpool. The guy was still whacking away. "Let's go get the book, Duke. Then we'll go see Bulloch."

We rode the elevator to the first floor. David wheeled me down the hall to a door marked X ray. After a moment he came out with the book. I put it under my behind and sat on it.

There was a policeman sitting outside Room 518, leaning back in a chair that was tilted against the wall, reading a book by Ed McBain. He was a young man, maybe twenty-four. He had on a clean, starched blue uniform. His shoes, belt, and holster gleamed with fresh polish.

I said, "Is that an Eighty-seventh Precinct book?"

"Yeah."

"We want to see Mr. Bulloch."

"Aren't you the kid he beat up?"

"Uh-huh."

"Why do you want to see him?"

"I want to see what he looks like, for one thing. He had on a mask. There's something I want to say to him too. He's allowed visitors, isn't he?"

He stood and hitched up his trousers with his elbows. He had a weightlifter's body and his shirt had been tapered to fit him tightly. "Yeah, he has visitors. I'll have to search you."

He patted David down. I gathered the sheet up from my legs and let it drop from my shoulders so that my genitals and the ledger were still covered. The policeman said, "Okay," and I covered myself back up. He unlocked the door and pushed it open. He said, "Do you want me to go in with you?"

I said, "No. He's going with me. I'll be all right."

He looked David up and down. "He's big enough. I've got to lock you in. Knock when you're ready to leave."

David pushed me into the room. Bulloch was propped up in bed, watching an old Bette Davis movie on TV. He turned to look at me. There was no expression on his face. He just looked at me and I looked at him. After a moment he turned back to the television. Bette Davis was smoking the hell out of a cigarette.

Bulloch was an ugly guy. His nose had been broken at least once and had a crooked hump in it. He had bulging, bloodshot eyes and a long pink scar along the left side of his neck. He turned back to look at me again, breathing in and out with a low-pitched rasp. His head was bandaged.

I said, "How you feel, Neal?"

He touched his bandages. "A little headache," he rasped. "How about you?"

"Legs are busted up."

Bulloch nodded his head, then turned away and reached beside his bed. He picked up a half-smoked cigar and stuck it in his mouth, rolling it around. He held the lighter flame a couple inches below the tip. When he got it going he took it from his mouth, looked at the tip, and exhaled a cloud of blue smoke.

I said, "Do you want to do some business?"

"What business?"

I leaned over, pulled out the ledger and held it up.

"Is that it?"

"Yeah."

Bulloch held out a hand. I gave the book to David and he took it over to Bulloch. He looked through a few pages, then handed the book back to David and puffed on his cigar, mouthing the end like a big, ugly baby with a nipple. He looked at me again. "You're not that tough."

"Yes, I am. You were overmatched."

"Bullshit." He looked back at the TV. The cigar smelled pretty bad.

"How much would your people pay for this?" I asked.

I waited while he smoked. He said, "How much do you want?"

I said, "I wouldn't take that beating again for a million dollars. I'll settle for less though. How high would they go?"

Bulloch shrugged. "Couple thousand maybe."

"Forget it. Come on, David. Let's go."

David turned my wheelchair around. Bulloch said, "Wait."

I nodded to David and he turned me around. Bulloch said, "Maybe they'd go higher. I can't say."

"Find out."

"Take a couple of days."

I shook my head. "When I go out the door I call the police. I don't want to fuck around for a couple days." I said *fuck,* because I thought it would sound tough, but it didn't come out of my mouth right and made me feel foolish.

Bulloch glanced at the phone. I said, "Ask them for twenty thousand. I'll take ten, you keep ten. I'll bring it up here tomorrow."

He glanced at the phone again, then stared back at the TV. Bette Davis was sucking on her third cigarette. He said, "Go outside. Wait in the hall for ten minutes."

I said, "Okay." David knocked on the door and we heard the lock click. The cop opened the door and we went outside.

I said, "You were great, Duke. I believe we've got him."

David walked down the hall and came back with three

Cokes in aluminum cans. I said, "Can you guys tell the difference between old Coke and new Coke?"

The cop said, "No."

David said, "A little bit. That new Coke is flatter."

I tried straightening and bending my right leg. It worked all right, but the knee felt creaky. The left leg did a little better. The toes on the left foot could wiggle just a little.

The cop said, "How come your legs aren't in casts?"

I said, "I don't know."

David said, "It's been ten minutes."

The cop let us back in, closed the door, and locked it. Bulloch was watching a commercial about heartburn. After it was over he clicked off the TV. "They want you to leave the book with me now," he said. "They'll bring the money in the morning."

I said, "No."

"That's what I figured. That's what I thought you'd say." He laid his cigar in an ashtray and felt around on his head. "I'll have your money tomorrow. Come up after noon."

"Ten thousand?"

The phone rang next to Bulloch's bed. He said, "Yeah, ten thousand." He picked up the phone and grunted into it. Then he put his hand over the mouthpiece and said, "Beat it."

21

THE DUKE LIFTED me back into my bed and asked what his next assignment was.

"Tomorrow," I said, "tomorrow we wrap up this little caper. Could you take me up there again, after twelve o'clock?"

Stienert came in the door on the run, almost knocking the Duke down. He was whistling through his teeth as he dialed the phone. "Stienert," he said. "Get hold of Baker for me." He put his hand over the mouthpiece. "Heavy stuff, Moon."

I introduced him to the Duke and they shook hands. Duke said, "I've already been sworn in."

Stienert frowned at him, then turned to speak into the phone. "Frank, get up to Moon's room. Do it fast. And we're going to have to get some federal people in on this. You know anybody at Treasury?"

Stienert listened a moment. I handed him the ledger and he looked through a few pages. "Get him up here too." He hung up and leafed through the rest of the pages. "Where you get this?"

"Came with the mail. It's an easy code," I said. "I figured out the first page. The rest should be easy."

He looked at the page I had decoded. "Let's do the rest of it." He looked up at the Duke. "What do you mean, sworn in?"

I said, "I gave him the oath, Moon. He's on the case. He helped me sucker Bulloch and we can depend on him. He's a

John Wayne man." I told him about the scene in Bulloch's room.

Stienert looked at the Duke and back at me. He shrugged.

I asked the Duke to get some coffee and orange juice and he walked out, rolling his shoulders and swaggering. I could almost hear spurs jangling.

Stienert caught on to the code quickly and wrote out a diagram. We divided up the other pages and began deciphering the messages. I said, "Who did Bulloch call?"

"Detroit. Phone is listed to a Theodore Williams. Detroit police are checking on him. Whoever he talked to agreed to twenty thousand for the book." He finished a page and looked at it. "Somebody getting ready to go to war."

"Yeah," I said. "Mine too. A guy in Rock Island, Illinois, with Laws Rockets, whatever that means."

The Duke came in with orange juice and coffee. I called him Pilgrim a few times and told him to be back at noon tomorrow. Stienert and I kept working on the pages. It was five o'clock.

Stienert answered the phone and wrote down information on a small pad he took from his jacket. While he was on the phone Baker came in with a dark-haired guy in a gray suit. Baker asked me about my legs while the gray suit paced around the room.

Stienert hung up and Baker made the introductions all around. The gray suit was Richard Gardner from the Treasury Department. He was a neatly dressed middle-aged guy. He had dark hair parted on the side and wore tinted glasses.

Stienert said, "This is the way it's shaping up: ERWA was collecting weapons, stolen military weapons, some of them. Holder kept the information in this ledger in some cockamamie code. Moon here broke the code in a couple hours. So Holder gets himself killed and the book disappears. Couple days later Bulloch shows up and thinks Moon has the book."

Baker said, "Did you have it?"

"No. It came in the mail this morning. I don't know who sent it." I passed him the note.

Stienert said, "Anyway, Moon had me tap Bulloch's phone and went up to his room with the book. Acted like he wanted to sell it and Bulloch tells him to leave the room for a few minutes. That's when he made his call."

Gardner said, "Who did he call?"

Stienert read from his pad. "Theodore Williams. Detroit cops say he's some kind of local crazy. Got some organization called Black Brigade that he's the head of. They're preparing for the great war of liberation or something."

Baker said, "Like ERWA, only black."

Stienert said, "That's the way it looks." He handed the decoded pages across the bed to Baker. "ERWA was building up a hell of an arsenal around the country."

Baker and Gardner read the pages. Gardner said, "We'll have to set up a raid, synchronized in each city, so we get them all before they can warn one another."

Stienert said, "Set it up tomorrow, sometime after noon. Little Moon is supposed to deliver the book to Bulloch tomorrow. Maybe you can raid the Black Brigade then too."

Gardner said, "I'm going to have to find a judge on Saturday night. I'll need nine warrants by morning." He looked at his watch. "Judges hate to be disturbed on Saturday night."

Stienert said, "Don't mention the tap unless you have to. It was illegal. Didn't have time to set it up."

Gardner said, "You're kidding, of course."

"Nope. I bluffed them at the switchboard. Taped the call and had Detroit police get me the rundown on Williams."

"Great," Gardner said. He started pacing again. "That's just great. All we need now is some sharp attorney to find out. All we need."

I said, "What's the problem?"

Gardner put his hands on the footboard of my bed. "Any arrests, any charges that result from an illegal wiretap or an illegal search can be thrown out of court. All inadmissible." He looked at Stienert. "You screwed up, boy."

Stienert said, *"Boy?"*

I said, "You've got the ledger. Won't that do?"

He shook his head. "Yeah, that'll do to nail ERWA and these guys with the weapons. Trouble is, we can't tie in Williams and the Black Brigade without the phone call."

Baker said, "Somebody has to deliver the money to Bulloch. Maybe we can follow him, pick up some connection."

Gardner said, "Risky." He paced around some more. "Who's in charge of this case?"

Baker said, "I am. Officially I'm in charge, but Ed and the kid have done most of the work."

Gardner ran his fingers through his hair. "That's great. A teenager in charge. And this guy"—he pointed at Stienert—"this guy has set it up so that we can nail ERWA but can't touch the Black Brigade. It makes me wonder if he's looking out for his brothers."

Stienert said, "Back off."

Baker said, "You're way out of line."

Gardner said, "Maybe. Maybe so, but I want him off the case. We can't afford to take any chances."

Stienert stood up, grinning. "You're crazy, man. You saying I can't stay on the case because there are blacks involved? Is that what you're saying? How about all you white guys? Can you be trusted to bust up ERWA?"

"That's different," Gardner said.

Baker said, "No it isn't. Ed's right."

Gardner said, "I don't care. It's a federal case now and I'm running it. He's off the case. I'm taking no chances with that soul-brother shit. I'll get the warrants and work with you and the kid from now on. Bring in some of my people."

I said, "Uh-uh."

Gardner was pacing again. "What do you mean, 'uh-uh'?"

"I only work with Stienert. If he isn't on the case, I don't go back to see Bulloch."

Gardner crossed his arms. "You've got to, kid. It's the only way we can legally tie in the Black Brigade. You've got no other choice."

"Sure I do."

"I can order you to do it," Gardner said.

Baker said, "You can't order a civilian to do shit. You know that."

Gardner breathed in and out through his nose and looked at us one at a time. Stienert said, "I think he's gotcha."

Gardner said, "What is it with you, kid? You and Stienert, you some kind of buddies or something?"

"Yeah."

"Some of his best friends are colored," Baker said.

"Wants Ray Charles for a neighbor," Stienert said.

"I like the way they can all dance," I said.

Baker said, "Natural rhythm."

Gardner shook his head. "Very funny," he said. "You guys have a great act. Real comedians."

I said, "Does Stienert stay?"

He looked at Stienert. "You better go with me to see the judge. And no more foul-ups."

"I knows my place," Stienert said.

They all stood up. Baker said, "I think we better put somebody in here with the kid tonight. Just in case they try to come for the ledger."

I looked at Stienert. He said, "Might be a good idea, Moon."

They started to leave. I said, "Hey, you guys. How about Holder? Who killed Holder?"

22

AT SIX THEY served supper and I ate while I watched a rerun of *The Andy Griffith Show*. Barney was giving Gomer a big lecture on gun safety and Barney's gun went off on him. I knew it was going to happen and I knew it was corny, but I went ahead and got a kick out of it anyway.

I called Vicki and we talked for a while. Stacy picked up the extension. "Vicki had a date last night, Chris. She said he was a nerd."

I said, "I think she is spoiled, Stacy. Once a girl goes out with me she starts throwing rocks at other guys."

"Modesty and humility," Vicki said. "That's what I like about you. Have you heard from Mote?"

"No, I haven't. What are you guys doing today?"

"I'm going to pick up Willa and play some tennis. We're getting to be pretty good friends."

"What do you talk about, you and Willa?"

Stacy broke in. "They talk about you, Chris. They talk about you all the time."

"What do they say, Stacy?"

"They say, 'Doesn't he have a cute—' "

Vicki screamed, "Stacy, shut up!"

Cute *what*, I wondered. Nose? Mouth? Smile? I said, "Vicki, would you do me a favor?"

"What?"

"Ask Willa to look in Leon's room. See if he still has the knife that Mote gave him."

"You don't think—"

"No. It's just something we ought to check."

"Okay, I'll ask her."

"I'll talk to you later, then."

"Okay, Chris."

Stacy said, "Cute little behind."

I could hear running footsteps and screams. I hung up and called Billy. He had to ask me all about how I was feeling before I could say, "Billy, we skipped a step."

"What do you mean?"

"With the knives. We just assumed that the killer got the knife from the shack."

Billy was quiet. I glanced up at the TV. Andy Rooney was complaining about junk mail. Billy said, "Yeah, we did."

"Make sure that your knife is still there," I said. "Then go over to my house. It should be in the back pocket of my fishing vest. Then go down to the hardware store and see if he sold any. Vicki is going to ask Willa to check on Leon's."

"Okay," Billy said. "Anything else?"

"Yeah, one more thing. Did you ever notice what a cute little behind I've got?"

"Too skinny," Billy said. "Wimpy-looking."

"Call me back tomorrow."

I flipped around the TV channels. Two channels had wrestling matches on. The other channels all had silly stuff on too. I picked up some magazines the nurse had left. I started an article about flying saucers but couldn't get interested.

I tried lying on my side. It felt good to get off my back. Fifteen hours to go before I met with Bulloch. I rolled over on my back and went to sleep for three hours.

When I woke up Johnny Carson was doing his monologue and Ed McMahon thought it was hilarious. Doc Severinson had on a funny-looking jacket.

Mote. I wondered what Mote was doing. He had acted very strange just before he ran back into the woods.

And who killed Holder?

One of the magazines had an article called "Test Your

Sexual IQ." I cheated on the test, marking the answers that I thought would score high, instead of telling the truth. I got a ninety-eight.

A commercial came on for chewing gum, the kind that identical twins chewed. The twin girls looked at each other and smiled identical smiles. Then identical twin boys came over and gave them identical hugs. I think they lived happily ever after, chewing that gum.

Twelve hours to go. I dozed off and on until about six in the morning then tried the TV again. All preacher shows. They each seemed to have pretty much the same message: If you don't give, we're going under.

I sat up and swung my legs over the side of the bed. It made me a little bit dizzy. I put my feet on the floor, leaned forward, and got big doses of pain from both legs. Dr. Gewertz had said four weeks before I could stand. What was I going to do lying around for four weeks? Maybe Vicki could come over. I could leave my sexual IQ test out for her to see.

23

STIENERT SHOOK me awake. "C'mon, Moon. Big day."

I sat up and Stienert handed me a tray with breakfast on it. I said, "How did it go with you and Gardner?"

"It went okay. We got all the warrants. Everything all set. We gonna wire you up."

"What do you mean?"

"Put a mike on you. Got a legal tap on Bulloch's phone too, trace everything coming in, going out, case he calls Williams again. The feds do things right, I say that for them. They think this Black Brigade bunch running drugs out of Florida. Suspect they robbed an armored car in Traverse City."

I said, "Did Gardner call you *boy* some more?"

"Once. He did it once and we talked about it."

I ate a piece of bacon with my fingers. "You know, yesterday, when you were talking with Gardner, you forgot to do your black English routine. You talked just like we do."

"So what?"

"So nothing," I said. "I just noticed, that's all."

"You just noticed, huh?"

"Yeah, I just noticed."

"You ever notice something and maybe just keep your mouth shut about it?"

"Hey, come on, Moon, I didn't mean anything by it."

"Maybe it's none of your business."

"Okay, it's none of my business."

Stienert walked over to the door and looked out. Then he closed the door and walked back to the bed. "They'll be here in a few minutes, Gardner and some other guys."

I didn't say anything. Stienert put his hands in his pockets and whistled through his teeth. It wasn't a song, he was just whistling some notes. "How's the legs?"

"They're better." I felt kind of shaky and my appetite was gone. I kept eating anyway.

"Good." He walked to the door and looked out. "They're setting up in the room next to Bulloch's. Tape recorders."

I nodded.

Stienert walked back to the bed. "You nervous?"

"Yeah, a little bit."

"Me too."

Gardner came into the room with another man. They each carried a suitcase. Gardner said, "We're going to record everything that goes on in there, so keep him talking if you can." Stienert walked over to the window and looked out.

I said, "You mean Bulloch?"

"Yeah. The longer he talks, the better. If he comes up with the ten thousand, tell him you want fifteen. See if you can get him to use the phone again."

"Okay."

"The more he talks, the better. Just keep him talking."

"What about?"

"Anything. The more he talks, the more of a chance that he'll slip up and give us some information. Just get him to talk. Make him mad, tell him jokes, insult him—anything."

The other guy opened a suitcase and took out some wires and a black box. Gardner said, "Tape the transmitter to his back and put the microphone on his chest somewhere."

Stienert walked to the door and started to open it. He pointed up. "I want to nail that mother, Moon."

I said, "Me too, Moon."

"Be okay it just ERWA and the Brigade getting ready to kill each other off. No big deal, they shoot each other—but it won't be like that. They ever get started, other folks get hurt."

"I know."

"They more than just crazies. All the guns they got, sooner or later they gonna start shooting."

At twelve o'clock we got on the elevator. David was excited and perspiring and he made me a little more nervous than I already was. There was a different cop outside Bulloch's door. When he saw us coming he turned to look down the hall. Gardner was standing halfway outside the next door. He nodded to the cop and gave me a thumbs-up sign. The cop nodded to us and unlocked the door. Bulloch was propped up, smoking another cigar and watching TV again. He looked at me, at David, then at the ledger lying in my lap. He held out his hand.

I said, "Where's the money?"

"Let me see the book first."

I picked up the book and handed it to David.

Bulloch looked at a few pages, then placed it on his lap with both hands over it. "Got a new deal for you," he said. "I keep the book and your mother doesn't get hurt, Burt."

"My mother—what do you mean?"

"Just what I said. It's simple. Give me the book and we let your mother go, Joe."

"Where is she?"

Bulloch shook his head.

I wanted to kill him. I wanted to jump on him and tear him apart with my fingers. I even started for him, but when I put weight on my legs, the pain brought me up short and gave me a moment to think. I remembered the microphone and transmitter. "Who's got her?"

Bulloch shook his head again. "In a few minutes you can talk to her." He glanced at the phone.

Gardner would be tracing all calls and recording them. I said, "Hand me the phone, David. And take the book back."

David handed me the phone. He reached for the book and Bulloch tightened his grip on it. "Take it, David. If he doesn't let you have it, hit him on the head."

David jerked the book away from Bulloch. I dialed my home number and listened to the rings. Everytime it rang I wanted to kill Bulloch more. My body was trembling. After four rings someone picked up and I heard my mother say, "Hello."

"Mom, are you okay?"

"No, I think I'm catching a cold, Chris. How are you?"

"I'm fine. Are you really okay? I mean, are you safe and everything?"

Mom sniffled. "Safe? Sure, I'm safe."

"Is anyone with you?"

"No. I thought I'd come over and see you later on, but I don't know. I wouldn't want to give you this cold."

I had happy goose bumps. "Mom, listen. Go somewhere. Go over to Billy's and wait there until I call you."

"What for, Chris?"

"Just do it, Mom. It's important. Do it right now."

"Well, all right. I don't understand though."

"Do it, Mom. I'll call you right back at Billy's."

"Okay."

"I love you, Mom."

"I love you, Chris."

I hung up and looked at Bulloch. "You son of a bitch."

Bulloch didn't say anything, looking straight ahead.

"It will be fifteen thousand now, scumbag."

Bulloch looked at me and shook his head. "Just hold on, kid. I'll be getting a phone call in a minute. You can talk to your mother then, Penn."

"I just talked to my mother. That's who I heard, nerd."

Bulloch looked straight ahead again. I dialed the phone and Billy answered. I said, "Is Mom there?"

"Yeah, she just walked in. How you doing?"

"I'm doing better. Keep Mom there, will you, Billy? I'll call you back." I hung up.

Bulloch looked at me, breathing noisily in and out. I said, "Fifteen thousand, thumbsucker. Yes or no?"

"Something's funny," he said. "Wait a minute. I'll get a call any minute and we'll make a deal, Neal."

The phone rang in my lap and made me jump. Bulloch signaled for the phone and David passed it to him. He said, "Yeah?" and listened for a moment. Then he smiled and held out the handset toward me. "Talk to your momma."

I said, "Hello." A strange male voice said, "Hold on."

There was some talking in the background; then a woman's voice said, "Hello, hello, who is this?"

The voice sounded familiar. I said, "Hello."

"Chris? Is this Chris?"

"Yes, ma'am. Who is this?"

"This is Mrs. Crowly. These men are here, these awful men. Why are they bothering me?"

"Are you okay, Mrs. Crowly? Have they hurt you?"

"No, but they've violated the sanctomy of my home. They want you to give them something. Why don't you give it to them, so they'll let me go?"

Gardner should be tracing the call. I wondered how long it would take. "I will, Mrs. Crowly. Just hold on a moment."

I put my hand over the mouthpiece. "You got the wrong person, Dumbo. You're not only a son of a bitch, you're a dumb son of a bitch. Your goons went to the wrong house, louse."

Gardner should have traced the call by now and sent some police to rescue Mrs. Crowly. Bulloch stretched out his hand for the phone. He said, "You be better off not talking to me that way. Might be a mistake to call me names."

I had a room full of police in the next room and the Duke standing beside me. I kept the phone in my lap. "You're sensitive, is that it? How can you be sensitive? You've got to know what a worthless piece of crap you are. What the hell good are you? You beat up kids, kidnap old ladies. Now you want me to talk nice to you, show you some respect. I wish I'd shot you when I had the chance."

Bulloch tried to look bored. He said, "Give me the phone."

I put the phone back to my ear. "Listen, Mrs. Crowly, there's a man who wants to talk to you here. Explain the theory of evolution to him, and they'll give your sanctomy back." I handed the phone to Bulloch.

He spoke into the receiver. "Put the man back on, lady." I could hear Mrs. Crowly talking to him. He held the receiver away from his ear. "Yeah, okay. Just put him back on."

Mrs. Crowly was still talking. I had to smile.

"Lady—" He held the phone away again and took a few of his sandpaper breaths. He covered the mouthpiece and asked, "Who is this?"

I said, "My least favorite person in the world, next to you. You picked the last person in the world to threaten me with."

"What's her name?"

"Crowly," I said. "Mrs. Crowly."

He spoke into the phone again. "Mrs. Crowly. Hey, Mrs. Crowly. Let me speak to the man and I'll tell him to let you go."

Mrs. Crowly gave him a few more licks.

Bullock said, "Uh-huh, okay, yes, ma'am. Okay, please let me talk to the man."

I looked at David and he looked at me. I winked at him.

Bulloch said, "You got the wrong woman. Let her go." He handed me the receiver and I hung up the phone. He said, "I can only go ten, kid. That's it."

"Nope. You called off the original deal, not me. Now it's gone up. Cost you fifteen, jellybean."

"Ten's all I got."

"Ten's not enough. The price is fifteen thousand, plus I want to know who killed Holder."

"I don't know anything about that."

"Somebody does," I said. "Whoever hired you, they must know. They must have killed him, trying to get the book."

"They never told me anything about that," Bulloch said. "They just told me Holder had the book and you took it from his house after he was killed. I don't know any more about it. Best thing for you to do is take the ten thousand. Nobody will bother you anymore. You got my word."

"That's real comforting, coming from you. I'm sure I can take your word for it, honorable man of his word like you.

It's fifteen, Maxine. Fifteen thousand and someone takes the fall for the Holder killing."

"No deal."

"Okay, let's go, David."

Bulloch said, "Twelve five."

I said, "Seventeen five. Either seventeen five or fifteen and the name of the guy who killed Holder."

Bulloch breathed some more. "You're getting on my nerves."

"What do you say when you go home?" I said.

"Huh?"

"When you go home. You know, your wife says, 'How did it go at work today, dear?' What do you say to her?"

Bulloch looked away. "Twelve five, kid."

"Class reunions must be great for you too," I said. "All those kids who never thought you'd amount to anything. Look at you now, Mr. Success."

"Twelve five and you better shut up. When this is all over I might decide to come for you again."

"Naw. Last time I took your gun away from you. Next time I'll shoot you with it. How about your mother? I'll bet she's proud of you. Probably tells all her friends about her wonderful son: My son, the thug."

Bulloch was breathing hard. He snatched up the phone and started dialing, ten numbers—long distance. Bingo! Bulloch said into the phone, "Hey, put him on." While he waited he felt around on his head through the bandages. He said, "It's me. Things went bad here. What I need, what I need to know to make a deal, I need to know who killed Holder."

I watched him while he listened. He said, "What's his name?" and I got chill bumps up my spine and the back of my neck. He listened some more. "Tell me what you do know. Everything."

The call was running into its second minute. Bulloch said, "What's an ERWA?" Then he listened some more. "The kid is holding out for more money. He wants to know who killed Holder and he wants thirty thousand." He glanced up at me.

After a minute he said, "I can't. He's got some guy with him, an intern. Some big, dumb-looking honkie with an earring."

David shifted his weight.

Bulloch said, "Okay," and hung up. "I can go fifteen, and that's it. Take it or leave it."

"Who killed Holder?"

"Some local guy. My people don't know his last name. Just his first name. Lyle."

"Lyle?"

Bulloch said, "Yeah, Lyle."

"Who is he?"

"They don't know. Just some guy who contacted them. Wanted to sell some information about guns some people had. Some bunch called Erga."

"ERWA."

Bulloch shrugged. "Whatever. This Lyle told them he could get them a list and they agreed to pay him. They heard back from him that you had it, the ledger. Fifteen thousand."

I said, "Sold."

Bulloch reached to the other side of the bed and lifted up a brown envelope. He took out three stacks of bills and put one stack back in the envelope. I gave David the book and he handed the book to Bulloch and took the money. They were hundred-dollar bills banded together in three bundles.

I put the money under the sheet. "Let's go, David."

David pushed my wheelchair to the door and knocked. A key rattled. David turned to look back at Bulloch. "You're dumb-looking too."

▲ 24 ▲

GARDNER WAS waiting in the hall. He said, "Nice going," looked at the money, and held out his hand. He told the policeman at the door to go in and get the ledger and Bulloch's red telephone. We followed Gardner into the room next door.

There were six guys in the room beside Stienert and Gardner, all talking on telephones. Stienert took the mike off my chest. "You guys were great. We already got the guys that had Mrs. Crowly. Right now they raiding all the places that got hidden weapons, raiding the Black Brigade too. I want to stay with this, Moon. I'll come by and see you in a few minutes."

I said, "Ask Gardner to come by too, will you, Moon?"

"Yeah, I'll ax him."

I started to say *ask* but caught myself in time.

Stienert said, "That's what you want, isn't it? You want me to ax him?" He was smiling down at me.

I said, "Yeah, ax him."

Stienert walked down the hall with David and me. He asked the cop for the key to Bulloch's room, unlocked the door, and pushed it open. He leaned against the doorjamb and talked to Bulloch. "Hey, bro. My name's Stienert. Anything happens to the kid here, I will find you and kill you. You hear me. I mean, the boy get hit by lightning, I come and kill you. He die in an earthquake, you die too."

David took me up to the sixth floor and lowered me into

the whirlpool. He took off his clothes and got in with me. "What's all this stuff about?" he asked.

"It's real complicated, Duke. Mostly, it's about whites hating blacks, and blacks hating whites. I didn't know there was that much of it going on."

"Was that guy really a Commonest?"

"No, Duke. He wasn't a Communist. I lied to you about that. I'm sorry. You really helped out and I want you to know that I appreciate it. I'm not really in the CIA either."

David sank down in the whirlpool so that the water came up to his chin. "Feels good in here, huh?"

"Yeah."

He sat back up. "I don't like that kind of thing, you know, hating blacks and the Ku Klux Klan."

"Me neither, Duke."

The Duke cupped his hands together and squeezed, squirting little spouts of water in the air. "Why do people do that?"

"I don't know. What do you think?"

He shook his head. "My dad's that way. He hates blacks, he's real prejudiced. I tell him, 'Daddy, not all blacks is dumb.' "

"That's a very enlightened attitude, Duke."

"Thank you."

I ate lunch and Dr. Gewertz came by to check me over. "Going to release you tomorrow, Chris."

"How long before I can stand?"

"Probably another three weeks, maybe four. I'll be coming around to check on you at home. I could cast your legs and ankles and you could clump around a bit. But you'll heal quicker just staying off them altogether."

"When tomorrow, what time?"

"Tomorrow night. I come back on at eight and I'll check you out one more time."

"Could I have another lunch?"

"Yeah. Are you still hungry?"

"Uh-huh."

"I'll get them to send up another lunch." He looked at my tray. "Do you like this food?"

"Yeah, I like it."

"You're not supposed to," Dr. Gewertz said. "Nobody's supposed to like hospital food."

A fat nurse brought me another big lunch. She said, "You should watch the news. It's all about you and all those guns and everything."

I turned on the TV and when the nurse left I turned it off again. I wondered about what Mote was doing. How did this Lyle guy get his knife?

While I was eating, Gardner and Stienert came in. Gardner said everything was going well with the raids around the country.

I said, "Would you do me a favor?"

"What?"

"The guy who went in there with me, would you send him some kind of letter or something? Something on official stationery, thanking him for his help."

"That goofy-looking guy? What for?"

"Just because he helped. Just to make him feel good."

"Yeah, okay." Gardner looked at Stienert. "Come on, let's go."

I said, "Don't you want his name?"

Gardner said, "What?"

"His name is David. David Standridge. You could send the letter here to the hospital."

Gardner said, "Yeah, okay. I'll do that."

"How about writing it down so you don't forget?"

"I won't forget."

"Write it down anyway," I said. "I'd feel better if you wrote it down. I know you've got a lot on your mind and might forget."

Gardner said, "Okay." He pulled a pad out of his coat pocket. "What's his name?"

"Did you forget?"

"No. I mean, how do you spell the name?"

"Just like it sounds," I said.

Gardner said, "Come on, spell it."

I spelled it for him. Stienert was staring out the window with his back to us. Gardner wrote down David's name and put his pad away. He looked at Stienert and said, "Let's go, Detective.

Stienert stepped away from the window, "Wait outside a minute."

"What for?"

"Just wait outside. Won't be a minute." He touched Gardner on the elbow and guided him toward the door.

Stienert closed the door behind Gardner. He walked back to the bed and pulled up a chair. "I'm not much good at apologizing, Moon." He turned the chair around and straddled it, resting his arms on the chair back. "But I think I owe you one."

I said, "Maybe I owe you one too."

He shook his head. "Naw, it was all me." He rested his chin on his forearms. "Gardner walked in yesterday and I knew he was . . . I knew he was going to call me *boy* sooner or later."

"How did you know?"

Stienert shrugged. "Just knew. He came in and looked at me and . . ." He sat up straight. "It's just something you can tell. I'd have bet money right then that he would call me *boy* before too long. Most of the time it's okay, but once in a while . . . every now and then I get so sick of it."

"Yeah, I guess so."

Stienert looked up. "Glad you didn't say 'I understand.' Can't nobody understand 'less they've lived with it."

"Yeah."

Stienert stood up and returned the chair to its original position. "So I apologize. I never got any of that, I never got that feeling from you. I shouldn't have snapped at you."

I said, "Don't you hate this kind of stuff?"

Stienert smiled. "Yeah, let's not do this anymore." He walked to the door. "I'm off the next couple of days. I come by and see you."

I said, "I get out tomorrow night."

"What time?"

"About eight, eight or nine, I guess."

"Want to do something? Go out and eat or something?"

"Yeah, Moon. I'd like to. Maybe you and Kate and Vicki and I could do something."

"You're on. I'll see you tomorrow."

I called Vicki's house and talked to Stacy for a while. She told me that Vicki and Willa were out playing tennis. I said I would call back. Mom's cold sounded worse and I told her to stay home and eat chicken soup. Billy and I talked for an hour, mostly about Mote and where he might be.

After a nap I called Vicki and made a date for tomorrow night. I told her about what had happened in Bulloch's room. She said, "Is Mote in the clear, then?"

"I guess so," I said. "I mean, they heard them say some guy named Lyle did it. I can't figure out how Lyle got hold of Mote's knife."

"Where are we going tomorrow?"

"I don't know. I can't dance. Maybe just go eat or see a show. I have to be carried around."

"I wish I could do it," Vicki said.

"So do I."

Everything was going great for me. Moon and I were buddies, Vicki and I had a date, Bulloch and ERWA and the Black Brigade were busted, my legs were healing, and the sun was shining. If only the Holder murder was solved and Mote was back.

Another nap. I remember hearing somewhere that your body heals fastest during sleep. I woke up at ten-thirty and watched the eleven-o'clock news with Rick Cantrell. The first ten minutes or so were all about the ERWA, Black Brigade, Bulloch business. They showed my interview with Rick Cantrell again and started to show the tape of the beating. I turned it off.

Then I turned it back on and watched it all the way through. It wasn't as bad to watch as I thought it would be. I wondered what had happened to Mote that was so bad that he couldn't remember it.

I slept great. One position all night, like a rock that had been dropped in the mud. After breakfast I took a nap until lunch. What a life. After lunch I made phone calls to Mom, Dad, Vicki, Leon, and Billy. Billy had heard from Mote.

"He's been upstate," Billy said. "He just got back and read the papers about all that's going on."

"How does he seem, Billy?"

Billy groaned. "Not real good. I think he feels bad about all the trouble you got in."

"Where is he?"

"Back at the river, downstream from where we used to camp. I think I might go down there tomorrow and fish a little bit."

I said, "That's a good idea. Tell him . . . well, you know what to tell him."

"See you tomorrow, then."

"Bring me some fish."

"Yeah, okay. Take care."

I did a job in the bedpan and really hated it. I rang the buzzer for an orderly and hated doing that too. Suddenly I began hating the whole situation. I wanted to fish or play tennis. Even walking to the bathroom would be thrilling. Good old self-pity. I wallowed around in it until Stienert came.

25

STIENERT CAME in pushing a wheelchair and grinning. "Got you some wheels, Moon."

"You're early."

"Yeah, Kate meeting us here. How you feeling?"

"Lousy. Terrible. I was lying here feeling sorry for myself, really getting into it too. Then you had to come in smiling and happy and spoiling everything."

"You feel better you get out of here." He sat down in the wheelchair and leaned forward. "You gonna love this, Moon. Yesterday we go back to headquarters and get Canzano on the computer. You remember her?"

"The policewoman?"

"Uh-huh. She a whiz on the computer. So she ask the computer for anybody last name is Lyle. Get a couple names. They don't look right for it, but we send some guys to check 'em out. She ask for everybody with first name Lyle. Get three. Two in jail, one in the hospital. So she ask for anyone with an alias. Lyle." Stienert shook his head. "Come up blank."

"Next thing we try middle names." He held up his index finger. "Get one Lyle. He arrested a few days ago." He leaned back in the wheelchair and grinned. "You ready for this?"

"Yeah."

"Arresting officer was Edward Stienert." His grin got bigger. "Assault. Parking lot, YMCA."

"Mr. Douglas?"

"Mr. David Lyle Douglas." His smile got even bigger and so did mine. "Can you dig it, Moon?"

"Yeah. Have you arrested him?"

"Can't find him. Wife say he didn't come home last night, but we find him."

"Then Mote's in the clear?"

"Almost. He still a suspect till we find Douglas, ax him some questions." Stienert got out of the wheelchair and stood by the bed. "You know, we big news—you, Gardner, me, and Baker. All this ERWA stuff, the Black Brigade and all—it's on the network. You probably get offers, be on Johnny Carson's show."

"I'd like to go fishing," I said. "Just camp out somewhere and fish all day with Mote and Billy. No telephones or TV."

Stienert said, "You ought to see ol' Theodore, that Williams guy, head of the Black Brigade. He's on TV, giving press conferences. Says this all a plot against black Americans. He says white men are Satan's angels."

He sat on a chair. "There's some white dude who is some kind of big shot in ERWA. He's on TV too, talking about this all a plot of the Jewish people—the Jews, the Communists, the nigras. He pronounce it *nigras*, almost say *niggers*, not quite." He shook his head. "You know something, Moon? I been watching those two guys, Williams and the ERWA guy. You know what?"

"What?"

"They doing the same act. I mean, if you could change their colors—make Williams white, the ERWA guy black—they could each do the other's job. Just change a few words. Wouldn't take them no time."

The door opened and Mote walked in. He smiled, "Hi, Chris," then looked at Stienert and nodded to him as he walked to the bed. "How you doing?"

Stienert stood up and looked at Mote. I said, "Moon, this is my uncle, my uncle Ralph. Ralph, this is Detective Stienert."

They shook hands across the bed. Stienert said, "I see the resemblance. I can tell you two related." He pulled Mote closer. "Way I can tell is you both got that same little crescent-moon scar under your eye."

Mote looked at me, then back at Stienert. Stienert let go of Mote's hand and drew his revolver. "You going to be trouble?"

Mote shook his head, "No, no trouble."

"You carrying anything, a gun or a knife?"

Mote pulled a sheathed knife from his hip pocket. He handed it across the bed. Stienert said, "I got to put cuffs on you."

I said, "You don't have to do that, Moon."

Stienert walked around the bed. "It's regulations. Still a murder warrant out for him. Murder suspect gets handcuffed."

"It's all right, Chris," Mote said. "How about cuffing me to the bed? Let me talk with Chris for a while."

"That'll be fine." Stienert handed Mote the handcuffs and Mote put one end on his left wrist. He snapped the other end around the side bedrail. Stienert put his gun away, walked around the bed, and sat back down.

Mote sat down in a chair. "How bad is it?"

"Not bad. Not as bad as it looks." I told him about Mr. Douglas. "How about you, Mote. Are you better?"

"Yeah. Much better. You know that nice stretch of water about two hundred yards down from our campsite?"

"Uh-huh."

"I bought some land there, three acres. Going to swap Mrs. Perry some work for the land and build a house on it."

"You going to live there?"

"Yeah. I'm not going to run anymore."

Stienert said, "We going to have to hold you in jail, Mote. You know that, don't you?"

Mote nodded. I said, "Why, Moon? How about Douglas?"

"We looking for him. Still, Mote a suspect. His knife. Have to lock you up until all this gets sorted out."

Mote said, "We'll build a cabin, you, Billy, and I, a bigger one this time. The land's in your name, yours and Billy's."

Stienert dialed the phone and talked into it quietly. After he hung up he said, "Baker be here to take you in, Mote. I told him take his time." He stood up. "I'll leave you guys alone, go get us some coffee. How's that?"

Mote said, "Black, thanks."

"Me too."

Stienert opened the door, "Sorry, Moon. You know?"

Mote said, "Are you worried about your legs?"

"No, they'll be okay. How about you? Are you going to be able to take jail?"

Mote nodded. "Sure, I took it before and survived. Yeah, I can take jail." He leaned closer. "You took quite a beating, didn't you?"

"Uh-huh."

"How do you feel about it, Chris? Can you remember it?"

"Sure, most of it. They keep showing it on TV and I didn't . . . I always turned it off when they came to the beating. But yesterday I watched it. It wasn't fun, but I'm glad I did it. It's like I'm through with that now."

"How do you mean, through with it?"

"I don't know, just through with it. I know it happened, I remember it happened, and I watched it happen and now, here I am."

Mote said, "Probably the worst thing that will ever happen to you."

"I hope so. How about your memory, are you getting it back?"

"Little pieces," Mote said. "Like a big wall there, but every once in a while I can see a little piece of it fall away."

Stienert came back with three coffees. We all took sips and I watched Mote's face crinkle up around his eyes.

"Mote, do you remember when Billy hit his thumb with a hammer and you made him experience the pain? Face it?"

"Yeah, I remember that."

"It was neat. I did that with my legs, lying here in the bed and it helped me get through it. I think watching the tape on TV was kind of the same thing. It helped to accept it."

Mote put down his coffee cup and held my hand. "Good."

"You don't know this, Mote, but when you talked about the feelings you had when your parents got divorced, well, that helped me too. There were lots of times when you helped me like that. Billy too."

Mote looked down at me.

"It was great the way you helped me remember how I got my scar. I think you need some help getting your memory back."

Mote chewed on his bottom lip. "I'll get it, Chris. It just takes time." He turned to look out the window.

"Come on, Mote. What's the use of building a house if you're going to sleep outside like a bunny rabbit?"

Mote looked back at me and smiled.

I said, "Crap in the grass like a beagle." He smiled some more.

I said, "What was it about the little girl?" and he stopped smiling.

He shook his head. "I don't know."

"You remembered something about a little girl when you watched Stacy down at the river. You remembered something and it shook you up. I could tell."

"Just a flash," Mote said. "Just a picture in my mind of a little girl, an Oriental girl. Then it was gone."

"What did she look like?"

"Just a little girl, dark hair, dark eyes, just standing there."

"Looking at you?"

"Yeah, I guess."

"Was she looking at you?"

"Yeah, she was."

"Looking up at you or down at you or what?"

Mote squeezed the corners of his eyes and rested his head on his hand. He spoke with his eyes closed. "Kind of up."

"Where were you? What were you doing?"

"I was, I don't know, I was just there, looking at her. Looking at her sad eyes."

"Were you standing or sitting or what?"

He shook his head. "I don't know, I was kneeling, maybe. Kneeling or squatting. Up in the air."

"How could you be up in the air?"

Mote opened his eyes and looked at me. "I don't know."

"Up in the air, looking down, kneeling or squatting. Was she to your right or left?"

"Right. She was on the right. I had to turn my head."

"How did you feel?"

"Scared. Jesus, scared."

"Was it hot or cold?"

"I don't . . . hot. I think it was hot."

"Who was the little girl?"

Mote gagged and swallowed. "She . . . her family was killed. She was just there all the time."

"Where?"

"Just there. She was just there, outside my cage."

"What cage?"

Mote took a breath and turned toward the windows again. I watched his face. His eyes were open but unfocused. After a moment he dropped his head. I felt scared. He reached over and picked up his coffee cup. His hand was shaking. He said, "Bamboo."

"How did you get out of it? How did you get away?"

"I don't know. That's all. The rest is blank."

"What about the girl? What was she wearing?"

He shook his head no.

"What about you? What did you have on?"

Mote looked down at his shirt, his pants. He shook his head no again. "I don't know." Mote pulled at his handcuffed wrist, glanced at me, then turned toward the window again. "That's the most I've remembered, the furthest I've got."

I said, "I bet if you got hypnotized . . ."

Mote turned back to me. "That might work. It would be worth a try."

I took a sip of coffee. My hand was shaking too. I said, "You know what, Mote? I'm scared."

"Scared of what?"

"Your memory, the part that you forgot. I'm afraid of it. It's like it's here in the room, some kind of invisible monster or something."

"That's the way it seems to me sometimes."

I felt a chill across my shoulders. "I hate it, Mote. I'm scared of it and I hate it. I can feel it. It's ugly and mean and evil. It's awful. No wonder you're so afraid of it."

Mote put his hand on my arm and I jerked my arm away. He said, "What's the matter, Chris?"

"I don't know, Mote. I don't know, I'm just real scared."

"Of me?"

"No." My chest felt tight and I had to force my breath. "Mote, I'm really scared."

"Why?" He touched my arm and I jerked it away again.

"I don't know. It's like your monster is after me too."

"It can't hurt you," Mote said.

"Yes it can. It really can, Mote. I don't know how, but it can. I'm afraid of it, like a nightmare."

Mote touched me again. I moved his hand away. "I'm sorry, Mote, but please don't do that."

I lay in the bed and shivered. Mote had tears in his eyes. Stienert stood up. I had forgotten he was there. He said, "You want me to call the doctor?"

"No, he wouldn't help." I tried to stop shaking and quieted down for about ten seconds, then it started again. "This is crazy."

Mote said, "Let's do it, Chris. Let's do it now, together."

"Do what?"

"The memory. Come on, I need you to help me get it."

"What do you want me to do?"

"Ask me some more questions about the girl, the cage, anything."

I said, "How about your scar? Do you remember how you got it?"

"No. It happened over there."

"Does it ever hurt?"

Mote shook his head no.

"Can you remember it hurting? Can you recall any pain there?"

"No."

"Try."

He closed his eyes, thought a moment, then said, "Nothing."

"Tell me about the little girl. How long was her hair?"

"Short. Bangs in front, short in back."

"Fat or skinny or what?"

"Kind of thin, slender. Her arms were skinny."

"What was her name?"

Mote shook his head, his eyes closed again.

"How far away was she?"

"A few feet. Four or five feet maybe."

"What does it smell like? Any smells?"

Mote took a couple breaths. "Yeah, like an outhouse."

"Urine?"

"Yeah. Urine and shit." He grimaced.

"How far away was the girl?"

"Not far. A few feet."

"She ever get closer?"

"No. Just that once."

"When was that?"

Mote was silent, head down, thinking. Then he gave a little jerk and touched his moon scar.

"What was that, Mote? What did you remember?" I suddenly stopped shaking. A warm glow started along my forearms.

He squinted his eyes tightly, making wrinkles. "Just once, her face was close."

"What about your scar? Did you feel something there?"

"Almost," he said. "Something, a little twinge. Now it's gone."

"Bring it back, Mote. Feel it."

I watched Mote's face. After a moment he shook his head slightly and said, "It's gone."

Before I knew what I was doing I leaned up on my left elbow and slapped him hard across his left cheek. He jerked back and grabbed my wrist. I reached over with my left hand and pinched the skin over his scar with my thumb and forefinger, hard.

Mote's hand shot out and grabbed my throat. He was squeezing hard, showing his teeth in a snarl. I pulled at his hand but he bore down harder. Stienert came running around the end of the bed. "Let him go."

He was lifting me as he squeezed. He let go suddenly and I fell back on the bed. Mote looked at me, then at his hand. I could see the ridges on the roof of his mouth when he threw back his head and let out a long wailing moan.

26

MOTE WAILED with his head thrown back for a long time, ending it with an "Oh, God" before he slumped forward. He put his head in his hands and sobbed. After a while he put his fingertips over his scar. He took his hand away and looked at his fingers, then wiped them on his shirt.

"A stick," he said. "She jabbed me with that stick."

Stienert turned, walked around the bed, and sat back down. I said, "What stick?"

"She always had a stick."

"Was she trying to poke your eye?"

"No, she just poked at me. She saw what I was doing."

"What were you doing, Mote?"

Baker came in and let the door shut softly behind him. Stienert held up his right hand, palm out like a stop sign. He put his left forefinger against his lips.

"I was . . . I'm on my left side, up close. Almost through. I'm chewing through the bamboo. Just a little more, a few more bites. She . . . I was going to take her with me but . . ."

His head was down. There were drops of sweat on his forehead and spittle at the corners of his lips.

". . . and she comes around and she sees what I'm doing. She's scared, she's more scared than I am. And then . . . and I've got her." Mote opened his eyes and looked at his own hand stretched in front of him. His hand was clenched into a tight fist and trembled. The veins of his arm stood out. His lips were pulled back, showing clenched teeth. "She smiled at me. I was choking her and she smiled at me. Then she was dead."

I looked at Stienert and pointed down at Mote's hand-cuffed wrist. He nodded and came around the bed, walking softly. He unlocked the cuff from the rail. He touched Mote's shoulder and motioned for Baker to follow him out the door.

Mote lay down on the bed, flat on his back. I turned on my side and watched him. He cried silently while his chest rose and fell. "It was the first time I ever saw her smile. She was always so sad, just standing there. I'd try to talk to her. She would just stand there until I started to go to sleep. Then she'd poke at me with her stick."

He closed his eyes and lay still for several minutes. I thought he had fallen asleep when he said, "The army psychiatrists called it PTSS—post traumatic shock syndrome. Said I had survivor guilt. That wasn't it, after all."

I said, "It was the girl, huh?"

"I guess. I guess I just couldn't let myself accept the fact that I killed a little girl." He turned to look at me. "Obscene, isn't it?"

I didn't know what to say. Stienert peeked in. I raised my head to look at him. Our eyes met for a moment and he nodded and closed the door.

Mote started to rise up. I said, "He'll wait, Mote." I turned over onto my back. Light through the venetian blinds made stripes on the ceiling.

Mote said, "I figure sixteen by twenty-four, with a sleeping loft."

"The cabin? Our new cabin?"

"Uh-huh. Big fireplace. We'll use rocks from the river."

I said, "How about a porch?"

"Yeah. Across the front, facing the river. Some rocking chairs, maybe a swing."

I could see it in my mind.

"And a tin roof," he said. "You know, for when it rains."

"Yeah, a tin roof." We listened to the rain on our tin roof.

Mote said, "Board and batten on the outside."

"Okay, and how about wood floors? Not plywood—real wood, like those wide boards."

"Pine, random length."

"With pegs in it?"

"Okay, we'll have pegs. What color should we paint it?"

"I don't know. What about a stain? Dark, like walnut."

"You sure you don't want Colonial Puke again?"

"No."

Stienert walked into the room. Mote sat up on the edge of the bed and rubbed his face, then stood up and held out his wrists. Stienert said, "Naw, that's okay."

They walked together to the door. Baker was waiting outside for them. Mote turned and winked at me before he walked out.

Dr. Gewertz came in and looked me over. He seemed pleased with everything. "Stay off your feet. I'll come by your house in about a week. Bring some crutches and see how that goes."

Stienert handed me my clothes. "Come on, Moon. Kate be here in a little bit."

I said, "I don't know, Moon. I really don't feel like partying tonight. I feel like I've played about ten tennis matches. Maybe you could just take me home."

"Up to you. I know that was rough stuff."

"Let me call Vicki, see what she says."

I dialed Vicki's number. Her father answered and went to get her. When she picked up I asked her if she would mind canceling out tonight. I told her about Mote getting arrested.

"Is Detective Stienert still there?"

"Yes."

"Chris, don't go. Stay at the hospital until I get there."

"Why?"

"It's . . . I can't tell you now, but please wait. I won't be long. I'll be there in a half hour. Please."

"Well, okay. But what is going on?"

"It's about the knife." She hung up.

Stienert slid my pants up and I zipped up my fly while he put on my socks. As he was lifting me into the wheelchair, Kate came in. She had on tight-fitting white slacks with a loose sweater and high heels. She bent over to give me a hug and I smelled her perfume. It was nice stuff.

She kissed Stienert and said, "Where are we going?"

"We got to wait awhile, wait for Vicki."

We waited. Stienert filled Kate in on what had happened. When the door opened I looked up and saw Willa. She stepped into the room and Vicki came after her. Willa stood with her head down.

She said, "My fault. It's all my fault."

I said, "What is, Willa?"

Willa turned to look at Vicki. Vicki nodded her head up and down. Willa said, "Mr. Holder, he told me in school, he said he wouldn't put Leon in no home, he wouldn't get Chris kicked out of school. He said if I come over to his house, he wouldn't do none of that."

She walked over to the window and looked out. No one spoke. Willa crossed her arms and turned toward us. "Mr. Holder, he had those papers. He showed me the papers and said I could have them. He said all I had to do was to be nice to him."

Kate said, "What do you mean, be nice to him?"

"He said I had to . . . he said he wanted me to beg him, get down on my knees and beg him. I said I'd do that, I'd beg him if that's what he wanted. But when I got down on my knees and he . . . he wanted me to do something else."

Kate walked over and put her arm around Willa's shoulders. "It's okay, Willa. It's okay to say it."

Willa started to cry silently, her shoulders shaking. She said, "He wanted me to—"

Stienert said, "He tried to make you perform a sexual act?"

"Yeah."

"And you resisted?"

"Uh-huh."

"Then what?" Stienert said. "Tell it all."

Willa shook her head and sobbed. "I said no and he had hold of my hair. I had Leon's knife but . . . but he took it away from me and laughed. I just ran."

An orderly came in, pushing a cart with sheets on it. He said, "I'm sorry, I'm supposed to get the room ready."

"We gone," Stienert said. He pushed me into the hall and the girls followed. Willa was crying and leaning against Kate's shoulder as we walked along.

In the elevator Kate said, "Do you have to arrest her, Ed?"

"I've got to take her in, get a statement."

We waited outside the hospital entrance while Stienert brought the car. Vicki held my hand, not speaking. Willa had stopped crying and was blowing her nose.

Stienert had the police car and he lifted me into the front seat. Vicki, Kate, and Willa got in back while he put the wheelchair in the trunk. Then he got in on the driver's side and sat behind the wheel, chewing on his lower lip.

"Better take you home," Stienert said. "Better take you and Vicki home first." He put the car in gear.

Kate leaned forward, her face close to the wire mesh. "It will be okay, won't it, Ed?"

He pulled out of the parking lot, driving slowly down a side street. "Willa, where did you get the knife?"

Willa said, "From their shack."

I said, "How did you get in?"

"I knew the combination from Leon's hat."

Stienert said, "Damn," and hit the steering wheel with the palm of his hand. "The morning you went to see Holder, is that when you got it?"

"Uh-huh. I was scared, going over there by myself. I wanted . . . I was scared of Mr. Holder."

Stienert said "Shit" very softly.

Kate said, "Will it be all right, Ed?"

"I don't know. Getting the knife. Getting the knife and going over there gonna make it sound kind of bad." He drove along slowly.

Kate said, "Where are you going?"

"Just driving around, got to think."

I said, "What if Willa says she had the knife all the time? What if she says that Mote gave her the knife a long time ago?"

"You don't go changing testimony, Moon."

"I know, but hell, Moon, Willa's not a killer. It's not like she's going to go around killing people."

"Yeah, I know." He turned his head to look over at a pedestrian.

"I'll say that I gave her the knife. I'll swear to it."

Stienert pulled into a driveway and turned off the headlights. He said, "I think that's him, Moon."

"Huh?"

He backed out of the driveway and picked up the radio microphone. "Code nine. I need backup. No sirens. Officer in pursuit." He gave our location and reached out the window to put his bubble-gum light on the top of the car.

Kate said, "What is it, Ed?"

"Rapist."

The man was walking along, fifty feet ahead of us. Stienert drew his gun and laid it on the seat. At twenty feet the man turned to look over his shoulder. Stienert turned on his headlights and blue light and the man started running.

Stienert sped up. "Stay in the car. Keep down and stay in the car, no matter what happens." He jerked on the emergency brake, jumped out of the car, and yelled, "Police officer. Halt."

The man ran between two houses. Stienert began running after him. I saw the muzzle of the rapist's gun flash. Stienert ran to the side and shot between the houses.

Dogs started barking and several lights came on. Stienert looked out from behind a tree and another shot came from between the houses.

I picked up the handpiece and said, "Detective Stienert is in a shoot-out. He needs help fast."

Nothing happened.

There were a dozen buttons on the radio and I didn't

know which one to push. I looked up and saw Stienert run between the houses. There were two more shots from in back.

Kate said, "Oh, God."

Another shot echoed from the backyard. I took the keys from the ignition, opened the door, and stepped outside, forgetting that my legs were broken.

27

I DROPPED the keys when I hit the pavement and they clattered over to the curb. I crawled over and picked them up, then crawled around to the back of the car. There were two more shots from the backyard. The second key opened the trunk. I had to lift the wheelchair to get at the shotgun. A man came out on his front porch and yelled, "Hey."

The shotgun was caught in the spokes. The man started down from his porch. "What's going on out here?"

Three shots from the backyard, then the rapist came running back between the houses. He ducked behind a tree and looked at me and the man from the porch, back and forth, back and forth. Stienert came running from between the houses and the rapist leaned around the tree and shot him from ten feet away.

Stienert turned a flip in the air and rolled toward me. I tore at the shotgun and heard the spokes snap as it came free. The rapist raised his gun in both hands, taking aim. I jacked in a shell and pulled the trigger, firing straight up. I watched him turn to point the gun at me. There was another shot and the rapist slammed back against the tree, then slid down, sat for a second, then fell to his side. He lay there and jerked like a dog having a running dream. Stienert kept his gun pointed at him until the police arrived.

In the ambulance Stienert and I lay on our sides, facing each other. Kate held his head in her hands. Her lips were pressed tightly. Vicki was sitting beside me.

Stienert rolled his eyes to look at Kate. "He dead?"

Kate nodded. Stienert closed his eyes and crinkled his face. There was a lot of blood soaked through the side of his shirt. He said, "You okay, Moon?"

"Yeah, I'm okay. You?"

A medic spoke from the front of the ambulance. "He's okay. He'll live."

Kate said, "He better." She stroked his cheek and sniffed.

I said, "Where is Willa?"

Kate said, "Baker took her in."

Stienert had his eyes closed. The siren wasn't as loud as I thought it would be. Vicki was petting my arm.

Kate said, "Ed?"

"I know what you going to say, Kate. Not now, okay?"

"I don't think I could stand it, Ed."

"We talk about it."

"You could teach. You'd be a fine teacher."

"I'm a cop."

"He'd have killed you if Chris hadn't shot when he did."

Stienert turned to me. "I told you to stay in the car."

"I'm sorry, Moon. I forgot."

"Next time I tell you stay in the car, you stay."

"Okay, Moon."

The ambulance took a hard right turn. Stienert said, "You a pretty good friend though, Little Moon. You know that?"

"So are you, Moon."

"Make a good cop."

"Not me," I said.

He closed his eyes again and spoke softly. "Been a cop eight years. Serious business." He opened his eyes again. "You unnerstand that, Moon? I'm very serious about being a good cop. I wan't serious, I be doing something else."

He was beginning to slur his *s*'s like a drunk.

Kate said, "We all understand that, Ed."

"Okay," he said. "All right, jus' so we all unnerstand."

I said, "There's a *d* in *understand*, Moon."

That made him smile.

▲ *EPILOGUE* ▲

THEY RELEASED Willa and Mote the next day. Detective Baker brought them to my house. Billy and Leon were already there, and we all sat on my front porch while Baker told us the news. Mrs. Crowly watched from her porch next door until I waved for her to come over. She waddled over to our driveway and stopped and looked both ways before crossing it. She sat on the swing next to Baker.

Baker said, "Douglas turned himself in last night. Him and that attorney fellow that was in your principal's office. They're saying self-defense." He sneezed and blew his nose.

I said, "How's Stienert?"

"Listed in stable condition. He's going to be all right." He blew his nose again and Mrs. Crowly got up and moved to the other side of the porch. She said, "You got that new virus."

"What new virus?"

"Aircraft, silver and black, for twenty-six years," she said. "They don't want to talk about it. Sky seeding the clouds with them new viruses to equalize the power, nation to nation."

Baker said, "Yeah, maybe so."

Mrs. Crowly said, "I don't want to catch it." She went down the porch steps and headed for her house. She stopped and looked both ways at the driveway again.

Leon said, "Too many books."

Mote stayed overnight at my house. He lay on the top bunk and we built the cabin together, starting with the foundation, and working our way up. We were building the loft when I dropped off to sleep.

In the morning Mote, Billy, and Leon left in Leon's car to begin work on the cabin. I watched from the front door. When Billy pulled away from the curb Leon cranked down his window, turned, and smiled up at me. I gave him a thumbs-up.

Billy's mom brought me a second breakfast every morning after Mom left for work, and Willa brought lunch around noon. Vicki had a summer job at a dry cleaner. When she got off she would come by and help Mom fix supper. Mom and the used-car salesman were dating pretty heavy and went out together most nights. His name was Robby and he was trying very hard to make me like him. I think they were making plans.

Baker came by every day and brought me up-to-date on the latest news. Stienert was getting better and the ERWA and Black Brigade members were busy telling on each other. Baker called them "peckerwoods." "Bunch of peckerwoods," he would say.

I had to go back to the hospital for X rays before Dr. Gewertz said I could walk without crutches. My shinbones had bumps on them and my leg muscles were shriveled and weak but I walked around some and it was wonderful.

Baker drove me down to the river. He never wore the wig anymore. When I asked him about it, he said, "Lost it."

We turned off the highway and onto the gravel road. "I got daughters," he said. "Three daughters. Every time we took a vote on the wig business it was four against one."

"So you just lost it, huh?"

"Yeah. Always four against one at my house." He turned onto the tractor road and I got my first look at the cabin. Two of the walls had been framed up. Baker stopped beside the oak tree. Before I got out he said, "If you want to you can call me Frank."

I walked around the car and we shook hands through the window. "Thanks a lot for the ride, Frank."

He said. "Keep your nose clean, Moon," and drove off.

We fell into an easy routine, working together every morning until it began to get hot. We waded the river and fished during the heat of the day, then after a nap, we worked on the cabin again until dark. Each day we could see the progress. After supper we would sit around the campfire, watching the flames and talking until we couldn't stay awake any longer. At night, I could hear the river.

On trips into town for supplies, I called Kate from the hardware store to check on Moon. She told me he was improving steadily. "Come visit us when he gets out," I said. "And bring Vicki."

Vicki said she missed me and made kissing sounds into the phone. I made kissing sounds back and two guys buying paint looked at me.

As the cabin neared completion, we began working harder and fishing less. Wading the river seemed to have helped my legs to heal, I began jogging every morning, first an easy mile, then two and three. The legs were coming back.

We were working fast, putting on the final paint one afternoon, when Kate, Moon, and Vicki drove up. After hugs and backslaps we went back to work. Moon found a brush and helped us while Vicki and Kate walked through the cabin making admiring sounds and discussing how they would decorate. We came to the final corner and Kate got her camera from her car. Mote, Moon, Leon, Billy, and I took hold of one paintbrush together and on the count of three made the final swipe. It is my favorite picture.

About the Author
CHAP REAVER

Herbert Reaver, known to his friends as Chap, is a chiropractor who lives and practices in Marietta, Georgia. He and his wife, Dixie, have been married for thirty years and have two grown sons, whom Dr. Reaver numbers among his best friends. His avocation is racquet sports. His addiction is writing.

Chap Reaver's writing has appeared in several humor and professional publications. MOTE is an Honor Book in the Eighth Annual Delacorte Press Prize for a First Young Adult Novel.